Binding Magic
An Obscure Magic Book 7

By

Viola Grace

Minerva enjoys her life as a master mage. She creates spells that no one has seen before and enjoys her family and friends. She will do anything for them, and she has.

Her side job is to act as an intermediary between extranatural races, and that is what she is doing the day that she walks into the dragon's den. Running from the dragon makes her confront her origins, and things get even more complicated from there.

Zemuel is an ancient being that owns lands and mines that contain strategic materials for other races. All he asks for an audience is that he be entertained by the envoy. Minerva has her work cut out for her. She really should have stuck to business only.

So, mate-hungry dragons, ancient gods and a surprising pedigree mean that Minerva's world just turned upside-down, and anchoring herself will mean surrendering a piece of her soul.

Chapter One

Minerva tidied up the dishes and heard her mother come through the door. She called out, "How was worship?"

Deirdre came in and smiled slightly. "Eventful." Her mother shook out her robes and took a seat at the table.

"Cup of tea?"

"Cabernet."

Minerva winced. "Right."

She poured two glasses and set them down at the kitchen table, sitting with her mother in silence.

Deirdre was a devoted follower of Hecate. It was a little peculiar, as she didn't have any magic of her own, but

Minerva had been raised not to mock anyone's faith.

When the glass of wine was nearly drained, her mother looked at her with helpless eyes. "I have been ordered to tell you where you came from."

Minerva blinked. "You adopted me."

"I did, but you weren't a foundling. Now, I know that you looked into your origins when you turned eighteen, but the files weren't precisely accurate."

Minerva hesitated. "What was wrong about my being found in the baby drop?"

Her mother cleared her throat. "It was part of a plan to get you into the official channels. Your birth was not strictly normal."

"Mom, why are you telling me this?" Minerva gripped her mother's hand.

"Because they want to talk to you. They need you to know what you are, so you will accept what they are."

Minerva was suddenly unnerved. "Who are *they?*"

"First, I need to tell you the story. After that, you can examine the documents and I will make the arrangements."

Minerva held up her hand. "Wait. I want to go to Benny's wedding tomorrow with a clear head. Can we wait for the big reveal until after that?"

"Yes. But they aren't going to wait long." Her mom smiled weakly.

"It will be the day after tomorrow or possibly tomorrow night if you are awake when I come home. We will get everything out in the open then."

Minerva came around to her mother's side. She gave her a hug. "I love you no matter what you tell me."

Deirdre smiled weakly. "My little amazon."

"You betcha. Now, get some rest, and I will see you after the wedding."

She smiled and stroked Minerva's

cheek. "How did I get so lucky?"

Minerva chuckled. "Like you always said, you prayed for me. Night, Mom."

"Give Benny and her guys my best."

"Of course. I always will."

Minerva finished her wine in one long gulp and washed the glass before she headed to her room.

The house was the one she had grown up in. Her mother had it built when she was a toddler, and it had included space for a small greenhouse and drying house. Minerva had a small lab in a shed, and inside the house, she had a serviceable magical library. The more complicated stuff wasn't in her home. She went to the Gangers' when she needed a specific or dangerous book.

The ward around her room flared as she entered it. Her life as a mage meant that occasionally she was hunted by those who wanted to use her, so it was her responsibility to keep herself and her mother safe from incursion.

If her mother had a secret to tell about her origin, home was the safest place to tell it. That night, Minerva was going to try and get some sleep. The next day was Benny's wedding, and she needed to be bright eyed and bushy tailed for the ceremony.

Minerva held a bouquet of magical flowers. They glowed with energy and had a dizzying scent.

Benny was linked and wedded to her three partners, and Minerva had never seen her happier. Freddy was nearby, and she looked to be gearing into flirting mode for the reception.

Minerva was the dutiful bridesmaid until she was alone after the main part of the reception. Folks were dancing and Ronathon, the goblin king, slid toward her. "Madam Mage, I was wishing to speak with you."

She looked into the moss-green eyes surrounded by swamp-green skin. "Yes, your highness?"

"There is a change of plans. We need you to go tomorrow."

Minerva blinked. "What? It was supposed to be next week."

Ronathon cleared his throat. "He changed the date of his audience. All of the others are scrambling to prepare their representatives."

She groaned. "I am going to have to take a portal. I wanted to take a plane."

Ronathon pulled at one of his pointed ears. "We will pay extra; we need that treaty and we need those stones. We have six months until our old defenses collapse, and it takes five to extract the stones. We don't have time to lose."

Minerva groaned. "This sucks."

"Zemuel is not inclined to throw more than one petition evening in a year. This is our last chance."

She pinched the bridge of her nose. "Fine. I will go. I will contact you in two days for my payment."

Ronathon blinked. "I will be there."

She wanted to hiss. "Yes, but don't stand too near me. Dragons can sense goblins, and they don't generally like your scent unless they are hungry. This is why you contacted me in the first place."

Years dealing with the Gangers and attending parties at their home had prepared her to work with non-humans, and Lenora and Emile regularly recommended her to their friends for intervention between the races. Taking on the goblins' need for territorial markers that would defend them against magical attack and wildlife intervention were a necessity.

Minerva looked around at those remaining at the party and sighed. For her, the evening was over.

Minerva found a corner to brood in, and Lenora came over to her.

"What is wrong, pet?"

"My mom and I need to talk, but the goblins need to move their meeting up. I am going to have to go out of town for a few days."

"She will understand."

Minerva chuckled. "It isn't that. She is going to tell me something that I didn't know, and we need to be together for that to happen. It has the hallmarks of one of those heavy moments in life, you know?"

Lenora looked over to Benny and nodded. "I know that feeling very well."

Benny was glowing and dancing with her mates.

Minerva could see the mingling of energies in the quartet, and the balance that was being struck would take a while to settle. Her initial binding magic was powering the union, and she felt a flicker of pride as she watched them move and dance around each other.

Lenora touched her arm. "You can come to us if you need anything, Minerva. You are family."

"Thanks, Lenora. It is appreciated."

"Well, now. Why don't you join the party again? Emile is looking for a dance partner and my feet are aching."

Min grinned. "That is because he usually has you off them."

"He is a demon in the sack."

Laughing, Minerva went in search of the incubus at the wedding. She owed him a dance.

Emile took her into his arms and swept her into a waltz with only a smile and the whisper, "When will it be your turn?"

Minerva shook her head. "I am not looking for a match or three of them. I am content to go through life as I have been, being useful and studying."

"Has the Mage Guild been after you?"

She chuckled. "No, they have barked up that tree so often that I have started turning the hose on them. I am not interested in wearing a uniform for the state."

"Fair enough. Your studies are coming along. You have a knack for spell creation that I have never seen before."

Minerva smiled at the compliment. "Thank you. I like it, though I have to remember to take notes as I go. It is like making a recipe that I have made a dozen times. When it is done, I just enjoy the result."

His smile in his green-scaled face was charming as it always was. If she hadn't created a dampening spell when she was a teen, she would have been obsessed with him. As it was, he was the father of her friend and the husband of her instructor. He was simply elegant, charming and very powerful.

They finished their dance, and she was spun away in the arms of another guest, so she continued the rounds, as did Freddy. It was their job as bridesmaids, even if it wasn't a normal wedding.

Ritual had to be upheld.

Chapter Two

Her mother was asleep when Minerva got home, so she left her a note and headed to her room to pack.

The goblins had chosen her because she met Zemuel's preferences. She was tall, curvy and powerful. He was more likely to grant her an audience than the goblins who had hired her.

Dawn was breaking and it was time for her to get going. She placed a few kisses and hugs around the house to surprise her mother and picked up her carryon. She sent a text to Zemuel's party planner, warning him of her arrival, and she got in her car.

The drive to the transport hub was

short, and there wasn't any traffic yet.

This was one time she really wanted a delay.

The arrangement for the transport took fifteen minutes, and she was sent across the continent in a matter of seconds.

Minerva stumbled as she left the platform. Having someone else transport her always felt weird, and having it happen three times in two days definitely threw her off balance.

She got clear of the incoming traffic and took out her phone, trying to scroll to the address so she could give it to the cab driver.

"Minerva Rogati?" A man walked up to her with a smile.

"Yes." She lowered her phone and looked at the gargoyle who was approaching her. He was either an accountant or a lawyer, but he was definitely a gargoyle, and she hadn't even seen one without a suit.

"I am Norman. I am here to take you to the manor."

Norman was the name of Zemuel's assistant on her correspondence.

She frowned. "I wasn't expecting you."

"Zemuel has been following some of your work; he wishes for you to have time to refresh and then join him for lunch if you are able." He reached out and took her bag from her. "Come with me, please."

She groaned and followed him out of the transport office and to the long silvery vehicle. A driver took her bag, and Norman held the door open for her.

She entered, and he closed the door behind her, walked around the vehicle and entered from the street side.

The driver tucked him in, and a moment later, they were off, cruising through the mountain paths, moving steadily upward.

She pinched the bridge of her nose. "How rude would it be if I begged off the lunch?"

Norman was surprised. "Do you have any reason for it?"

"I just found out about this change yesterday, at one of my oldest friend's weddings. I have not yet been to sleep, and as I understand, the audience petition lasts into the wee hours; I need sleep."

Norman chuckled. "Understandable. Of course. I will notify him, and he will not hold it against you, I am sure."

She sighed. "This is not turning into my day."

Norman patted her hand. "It will be fine. He is not vindictive."

Minerva laughed. "That is not what I have heard."

Norman smiled, and their vehicle continued to twist its way into the mountainside.

The dragon's manor was a lair built into the side of a cliff face like the ancient city of Petra.

She could see the smoothly carved pillars of stone as they approached. When the vehicle stopped, the driver opened Norman's door, and he came around to open hers.

Her bag was whisked away from her and into the elegant cavern in the cliff.

Norman took her hand and helped her out of the transport, leading her into the structure that had been crafted out of the local stone.

The interior had the ambience of a hotel without the front desk. Couches, low tables and bars were around the huge entry chamber.

Norman spoke softly. "Sound echoes here, so this is the chamber of communication."

Minerva looked around casually and

saw a few familiar faces and several unfamiliar species. Everyone was milling around with their gazes on a nondescript door connected to a long tower.

"I am guessing that it rises to his personal quarters?"

Norman nodded. "He uses it only when he has guests."

To answer her next question, the door opened silently, and a dishevelled blond elf stumbled out and into the arms of her people. She gave them a nod, and the men grinned, congratulating themselves. Sex for favours was not concealed in the extranatural community.

Minerva looked the woman over and determined that the favour she had offered was a blowjob. There was redness around her lips and her legs were firmly together, so penetration had not occurred. It was a good thing to note. She wasn't offering Zemuel her body, but knowing what he was likely to ask for was a bit of information that would change how she interacted with him.

If Zemuel were ruled by a sexual urge, it would make her method of negotiating a little more overt.

"Mage, please come this way." Norman looked a little flustered.

She grinned. Gargoyles had a prudish streak that popped up now and then. Apparently, Norman was in that particular mood.

A second, more ornate, elevator took her upward, and she swayed. She was nearing the edge of exhaustion. Either she could cast a spell for energy that would knock her out for a few days when it had run its course, or she could take a nap. Minerva was voting for nap.

"Mr. Norman? What is the local time?"

"Oh, it is nine in the morning. The cocktails will begin at seven in the evening, and he will take up his throne at eight. After that, he will select those al-lowed to try and win a petition for three hours. Then, he hears the petitions and everyone is dismissed immediately after, somewhere around four in the morn-ing."

The elevator chimed, and the door opened on her floor. Well, it was also her room. The elevator opened into the guest suite.

Norman escorted her inside, his wings folded against his back. "All amenities are here; you have a balcony, a fireplace if you want it. The tub is filled in under a minute, and there is a robe for you. Your bag has been unpacked, and if you like, we will give you a call be-fore the cocktails begin."

She glanced at him. "Do the goblins have a similar suite?"

He chuckled. "They are not allowed to remain on the premises. If they can make it here before the cocktail hour, they will be allowed in. At the stroke of seven, the doors are locked for new entries."

She checked her phone. "There's no signal."

"No, he has never seen the need for one, so we don't have a tower. Your connectivity will resume the moment that you leave the mountains." Norman paused. "Do you have any other questions?"

"I would like a wakeup call at six if that isn't too much trouble."

"Of course. I will have it registered. Enjoy your stay and your rest."

She nodded. "Thank you. See you later."

Norman returned to the elevator, and she was alone.

The remote for the drapes had instructions attached, and she closed them, revelling in the dark cocoon that was created.

She stripped and crawled into the bed, her clothing draped over the foot. She set her alarm for eight hours and placed it next to her head.

It said a lot about her life that she simply dropped into sleep without another thought.

Zemuel watched the monitor and turned his head as his assistant came in. "Well, she actually did want to sleep."

"Last night was Beneficia Ganger's wedding, and Minerva was a member of the bride's party. She looked tired."

Zemuel nodded. "She did." He drew a clawed finger along the curve of her cheek on the display.

It was as if she could feel it. She muttered in her sleep and turned to her side, exposing the pale curve of her back and hips as the sheet shifted.

He smiled and trailed his finger down that sensuous curve. "She is magnificent."

"Sir, if I may?"

"Speak." Zemuel scowled.

"She was in the entry chamber when your earlier—uh—companion came down. Her expression indicated disgust with the situation."

His moment with the elf had nearly been forgotten. He had granted their request for limited mineral rights within their demesne, and she had insisted on thanking him with her mouth. It had not been a difficult decision, and his contact with her had been to stroke the froth of her hair.

"Fuck. That is going to make things awkward." Zemuel had been researching the woman on the screen for a year. Her body made his mouth water, and his senses were on peak alert when he saw the CCTV recordings of her in the park, opening the gateway to the demon zone. It had taken a lot of influence and more money to get the recording deleted from systems across the country.

He knew his mate from the moment he had first laid eyes on her. His collection of magical anomaly videos had shown him Minerva in all of her glory.

Once he had her *scent,* it had taken a year of waiting to find a situation that would bring her to him. That moment was here.

He would be able to smooth over the elf and her service if Minerva asked. He doubted that she would comment on it. She had been around the extranaturals most of her life. Sex and magic were traded for power all the time. Some races used it as standard currency.

Norman cleared his throat. "I do not feel it is appropriate for you to be watching her. She is a lady, a mage and a respectable woman. Dignity in every bone of her body, and this kind of peeping is an invasion of her privacy."

Zemuel raised his brows in surprise. "You are standing up for her?"

"She is asleep, so she needs someone to do it."

Zemuel grinned and turned off the camera. "So, she already has a champion. Interesting."

"She is an interesting woman and deserves to be treated with respect."

"Fair enough. I will speak with her this evening." He smirked. "What shall I have her do?"

He could see that Norman was going through a dozen or more of the creative events that Zemuel had insisted on over the decades since he began this process.

"Have her sing. She has a good voice, and it is unrelated to anything else that she does. If you gain her cooperation and keep her, you need to see how she will perform in public."

He nodded. "Excellent point. Make sure that you draw singing from the bag when the time comes."

Norman inclined his head, and his wings came out slightly. "Yes, my lord."

Zemuel looked longingly at his monitor but decided to get to work on the new tower. He flexed his hands and the claws extended.

He left the media room and walked out to the balcony. He opened his wings and launched himself into the hollow cavern. He soared in the darkness of his domain and used the feel of the rocks around him. Smiling to himself, he went to the hidden fresco that he was working on, carving the image of her smooth back into the stone. Curls of granite fell to the distant cavern floor far below.

Once that was done, he worked on what he considered to be his weekend cottage. He had already carved out the staircase, and now, the wide-open floor space needed finishing. He had time to spend before the evening's festivities and clawing his way through stone would keep him from thinking about flying to Minerva's quarters and peeling back her sheets.

He needed to wait on that until they had been properly introduced.

After they were together, he wanted everything she was willing to give.

The wakeup call had come while she was getting out of the shower. As fun as the tub looked, it wasn't quite the day to enjoy it.

Minerva dried off, wrapped a towel around her and brushed her hair. There was no hair dryer, so she whispered a small spell and her hair curled and cascaded softly down her back in precise waves.

It was the easiest part of her ritual to get ready.

She sighed as her stomach growled. Cocktail hour on an empty stomach was going to be tricky, but she had a few hours to figure it out.

Her clothing selection was the first thing she had put on her bed when she had slipped from the sheets, and as she pattered around in bare feet, the snug corset taunted her.

It was appropriate to wear aspects of ancient clothing traditions when confronting an ancient being. The corset was an evergreen.

A little exploration turned up a fridge stocked with alcohol and soda. She opted for the sugar and turned to take stock of the room.

The rush of magic in her vicinity came a moment before the tray of sandwiches and fruit arrived. After them, a pot of coffee and accessories appeared on the bar counter.

Sighing with relief, she tucked in and worked her way through the food. She hadn't had anything since the reception the night before and magic burned a lot of energy.

When she had eaten and had the blessed coffee, she got dressed in a billowing silk dress and the corset. After she had closed the busk and laced the corset into place, she adjusted it and tightened the laces again. She folded the skirt into even pleats around her, and the black fabric contrasted with the gold embroidery on the black corset. She and her considerable assets were now encased and displayed.

Time for makeup.

With an evening of socializing ahead of her, she paid special attention to fixing her makeup in place. When she was done with the final touches, she looked into the mirror and placed the mage mark on her cheek so that those she spoke to would not take her for helpless. When you were the only human in a room full of extranaturals, you had to make it plain that you weren't a target.

By the time she stepped into her shoes, it was six fifteen. She walked out onto the balcony and stared into the mountain range. It was a good place to meditate, and when her phone chirped again, she snapped out of her reverie and headed to the elevator.

She did not know how many petitioners would be at the party, but she had agreed to do the talking, so she pressed the button.

To her surprise, it arrived right away and swept her to the main floor in decorous style.

As she looked out into the lobby with faces turned to see who was emerging, she fixed her dignified expression in place and stepped onto the polished stone. *Showtime.*

Chapter Three

$\mathcal{M}$inerva was stopped before she had gone three feet. She turned her head, and the elf who was sliding his arm around her froze in his tracks.

She looked at him coldly. "Do I know you?"

He pulled his hand back. "No, Mage. Pardon. I had no idea who you were."

She inclined her head. "Prince Ekrodian, your judgment is usually not so poor."

He blinked and his rainbow eyes widened. "Have we met?"

"Only once. Corudet City."

His porcelain skin flushed, and he looked from side to side. "Did you…"

"I did nothing. I was not there to observe; I was there to help a friend." She smiled tightly. "I did and got the fuck out of there."

"May I ask your name?"

"You may. I am Minerva."

"Thank you for your kindness and discretion, Minerva. May I get you a drink?"

She mentally rolled her eyes. "I will get it myself. I will need to leave the elevator entrance eventually."

He nodded. "I will accompany you."

She moved past him and swept to the bar. The bartender moved with the grace of a shifter and came up to her with a smile. "What can I get for you, magnificent mage?"

She smirked. "A shot of peach schnapps and pineapple juice over ice, please."

The man moved with dexterity and flipped the bottles around until the curved glass was filled, and he then propped a cherry on top.

She laughed. "That is optimistic."

He grinned and a cackle came from his lips. She recognized the call. He was a raptor of some type. There must be an aerie community nearby.

"Thank you, kind sir."

He gave it to her with a flourish.

Minerva smiled and went to mingle with the rest of the petitioners. Even humans were represented, which was rather brave of them.

She wandered over to the humans who were huddled around with their glasses clutched in their hands. Word of Zemuel's preferences had obviously gotten around, but based on the women who were dressed to seduce, they had missed a memo. The women were both tiny and frail.

Even the elf from earlier had been tall.

The leader of the group asked her, "Excuse me, Madam, but are you human?"

She quirked a smile and sipped at her drink. "Yup."

The entire party relaxed.

She heard about the new road they wanted to build and what the girls were willing to do to get it.

She sighed. "Does anyone in your party have entertainment skills? Zemuel has a tendency to ask for folk to humiliate themselves in order to get an audience."

The leader stiffened his spine. "We can do that. What will he ask?"

"The lot is drawn by his assistant. The exhibitions are inside the bag. It is ostensibly random." She was about to tell them more but a wall opened and a throne room was exposed.

Her sense of time was skewed without seeing the sun, but if the door was opening, she would walk through it. The humans were on one side of her and the elves on the other. The additional races moved toward the doorway as one, but Minerva hung back.

A familiar voice spoke from behind her. "Changing your mind?"

She smiled slightly but kept her gaze on the backs of the other petitioners. "No, Mr. Norman. I have changed it both ways a thousand times. I am just waiting to make an entrance."

He chuckled. "We can work with that. If you will do me the honour?"

He extended his hand to her, and she placed her palm on the back of his rough knuckles. He was still a bit taller than she was, so she was sure that they made a striking couple entering the throne room.

He led her through the crowd to a spot directly in front of the throne. "Stay here until you are called."

She nodded and lowered her free hand to her side. She sipped at the cocktail in her other hand, and soon, there was another gong and the sound of huge wings pulsed through the air.

Zemuel dropped to the floor in front of the throne, his wings nearly twenty feet in span.

Minerva took it all in. His silver skin, the bare feet and loosed draped fabric drawn up and pleated to form trousers were the initial impression. The long black hair in a thick braid matched the dark brows that winged over his deep pewter eyes.

She absently noted the sharp blade of his nose and the slash of his lips. She didn't feel comfortable with further examination. He was staring at her.

Being examined by an eight-foot predator in his natural habitat was a little intimidating, but she had a job to do.

Zemuel settled his wings behind him

and settled onto his narrow-backed throne.

"Norman, what can these folk do to lighten my evening?"

Norman took his place beside Zemuel, and he cleared his throat, removing a bag from his belt. "I believe that they have expressed willingness to entertain you."

Zemuel clapped his hands together. "Excellent. Let's begin."

The clap of his hands was like thunder. Everyone in the room jumped, but Minerva had been expecting it. She sipped at her cocktail.

"I believe that the elves wish a second interview with me. They shall go first."

Norman reached into the bag and pulled out a small piece of slate.

"My lord wishes you to breathe fire." Norman chuckled.

Zemuel smirked. "For those mages in attendance, magic will not work in this chamber."

Idly, Minerva looked around the chamber and spotted the bar. It was another bartender, but this one had giant in his blood. He winked at the eye contact.

The elves frowned and muttered among themselves.

Norman cleared his throat. "If they cannot perform the task, anyone else who wishes to perform it can win their interview."

Minerva thought about it for another two minutes. With a sigh, she went to the bar, asked for a glass of vodka and a lit candle.

She walked back to her spot in front of Zemuel, slurped up the vodka and sprayed it out in a fine mist over the candle. The blue flare of flames with yellow edges cascaded out over eight feet.

When she was done, she wiped her mouth with the back of her hand and returned the glass and the candle to the bartender with thanks. He winked and put them away.

The liquid paraffin he had given her in lieu of vodka had definitely been impressive, but now, she had to deal with the consequences.

He poured her some mouthwash and gave her a metal cup. "I think you might need this."

She grinned and swished and spit. "Thank you."

He inclined his head. "We are always ready with the implements, but few think to ask."

She returned to her spot and found it occupied by the humans. She shrugged and went to the back of the gathering. The elves left. Their chance was over.

Norman looked displeased, but he dug in his bag for the next task.

"The human contingent will perform a juggling act. As there are many of them, two members must juggle."

Minerva stood in place and watched as they frantically tried to juggle anything and everything.

Zemuel watched them with a scowl. It appeared that he was not impressed with their efforts.

Norman once again called out, "If anyone can perform this task, they can have an additional interview with Lord Zemuel."

After a few clumsy attempts from the other contingents, Norman made eye contact with her.

She headed to the bar and asked for lemons.

He grinned and handed her three. Once again, she took the front spot. She juggled the citrus for a minute, and then, she stopped, bowed and returned them to the bar.

Zemuel appeared amused when she returned.

"The goblin contingent is required to sing."

The crowd looked around in confusion, but Minerva stepped forward. It was funny. Goblins didn't sing in any way that the human ear found acceptable. Demanding it of them was a joke.

"Any particular song or style?"

Zemuel raised a brow. "Ancient Hynerian."

She frowned. "That is a little tricky."

"Can you do it, or do you forfeit?"

She opened her mouth and wailed a long, keening note that preceded her beginning to turn and twist to her own beat. The Hynerians were one of the first nations of extranaturals to gather in their own defense. They were of such different origins that movement became part of their language.

She used her body to speak of longing, justice, fear and power. When she was done, she ceased her song with a snap and inclined her head.

He cocked his head and leaned forward. "You confused the word heat for desire, but it was otherwise a well-performed song."

She inclined her head, and the bartender delivered another cocktail. She could feel the pressure of her corset and the sweat that dampened it. The silk of her skirt stuck to her legs.

Minerva stood where she was and enjoyed a few more cocktails as the groups tried to perform the tasks. The unicycle for the dwarfs was a bust, as was the crochet exam for the giants. They had not brought the right representatives with them.

Minerva thought about it, and she was hungry again. Too bad there was no food on offer.

Zemuel suddenly waved his hand. After two hours of tomfoolery, he had had his fill.

"Well, Madam Mage, as you are the only one to have won an interview, my time is yours. Shall we discuss things over dinner?"

She looked behind her and the crowd was gone. One by one, they had left as their attempts to carry out the orders had failed.

"Well, this is embarrassing."

Zemuel walked up to her and extended his hand. To her amusement, he shrank until he was only six inches taller than she was in heels.

She slid her hand into his and then held her breath as his wings flared wide and he flew them upward.

When they reached a balcony that had been invisible from the main floor, he set her on her feet as if it had been the most natural thing in the world.

He led her inside.

She smiled. "Thank you for reducing your height. I am used to being taller than most folks I speak with. Looking up was giving me a crick in my neck."

A table for two had been set, and the covered dishes spanned from one end of the eight-foot expanse to the other. It seemed that Zemuel was the measurement standard for everything in his home.

He led her to a chair at one end and held it for her, settling her in.

He crossed to the other chair and tapped his fingers on the table. The dishes rose up and began a slow path around the table itself.

Well, that was one way to serve yourself. As she reached for a dome, it lifted and the serving utensils were under it.

She took a small portion of each food item, and the dishes settled.

Zemuel smiled. "Well, now that you have me alone, what do you want?"

She looked at him and stated, "I am here to petition on behalf of the goblins."

"Why? I haven't eaten any in centuries."

"That is not their concern. You are in possession of mines that yield the mineral used in their warding system. They need a new supply of those minerals. That is what they are asking for. Will you supply them with the stone they need?"

He smiled slowly. "What are they willing to pay?"

She nibbled at a carrot and the negotiation was on.

Chapter Four

After hearing the offer, Zemuel nodded. "Deal."

"Just like that?"

He grinned. "Just like that."

He extended his hand, and a data pad flew from somewhere within the room to smack into his hand. He tapped a few markings and nodded. "Done."

"That was anticlimactic."

He grinned. "It usually is. Requests to bring in magical weaponry usually have more details in them, but defenses are fairly easy. They can come to the mine tomorrow, and the boss will show them around and give them the options of shape."

She blinked. "Weapons?"

"Did you not know? I am the largest importer of magical weaponry on the continent." He leaned back and smiled. "I would have thought you had done your homework on me."

She shrugged and focused on her meal. Flicking her glance up cautiously when she thought it was safe, she met his amused glance. "I am here as a representative of the one goblin nation. It isn't really my speciality."

He rolled his wineglass between his finger and thumb. "Why did they ask you?"

She shrugged. "I was informed that I have characteristics you would find attractive."

His smile was definitely amused. "What characteristics are those?"

"Height, figure and power." She kept it blunt.

The laughter rang and echoed in the

chamber. The column of his neck flexed, and his elongated canines were definitely visible as his wide jaw moved with the laugh.

She continued to work her way through her food until she was finished. She set one hand in her lap and picked up the wineglass.

"So, you were selected to seduce me?" He leaned forward with interest.

"No, merely get your attention. I don't seek out men for money."

He inclined his head. "Apologies. I am merely struck by the ease with which you could accomplish your goal."

For the first time in quite a while, she blushed. The barrier of the table was a comfort, because his gaze said he didn't want it in the way.

Idly, she tried to use a small spark of magic in her lap, and he looked at her sharply. "What are you attempting to do, Minerva?"

She shrugged. "Just testing to see if the no-magic zone extended this far."

"It does."

She inclined her head. "You can understand that I had to test it."

He frowned. "Yes, I suppose I can. Did you learn what you needed?"

She smiled. "I did. Thank you."

Minerva learned that her magic did work; she just needed to put some extra power into it.

He finished his meal and tapped the table twice. The food disappeared.

"Enchanted stone?"

Zemuel nodded. "Very perceptive. You are indeed what was described."

She made a face. "I do not want to know."

"Oh, but I want to tell you." He waggled his brows.

She looked at the expanse between them and was at a loss for conversation.

"Is there anything you want for yourself?"

Minerva wrinkled her nose. "Not particularly. Perhaps a tour of your home."

He grinned and got to his feet, walking around the table and gripping her chair. "Lady, if you would do me the honour."

She arranged her skirt and got to her feet, setting her hand on the back of his as he walked with her into the distant shadows of the chamber.

A wide corridor was cut into the stone, and she could feel the touch of the cool evening air. The floor was smooth under her feet, the slight click of her heels was the only sound and it echoed as she walked.

Her voice was quiet when she observed, "You enjoy sound."

He chuckled, and that sound was magnified and echoed around them. "I do. When you sleep underground, sounds from what is going on above is essential to knowing how the world is changing."

"You do have a very adept grasp of technology."

"Thank you. I find the more recent discoveries and equipment to be most useful." The rough, deep gravel of his voice sent shivers down her spine.

She couldn't stop herself. She asked, "You have been here a while?"

"I have slept under this mountain for nearly a thousand years. I woke and carved the stone into this place four hundred years ago when the wave of magic woke me."

She shuddered. "That was a large one."

"It was. It created enough of a magical population for me to surface and ply my trade."

"Selling magical weapons."

"Well, the unpowered have an inborn hate for those extranaturals around them."

Minerva frowned, thinking of her mother. "That is not always the case."

"It is more common than the exception."

Weak light began to spill into the corridor, and as they closed on the origin of fresh air, she gasped.

He continued to walk with her out onto the wide plateau carved into half of a mountain. It was a monstrous expanse of stone with claw marks gouged into the stone, denoting the size of his other form.

She shivered at the thought of the magical creature who was leading her into the centre of the landing site.

"I like to come out here and watch the stars dance."

There was something so ancient and sad in his tone. She moved closer to him and looked up and out to see the stars as they hung motionless. A shooting star skidded across the sky, and she closed her eyes to make a wish.

Zemuel slid a hand into her hair, and she felt his lips press against hers. He was careful and deliberate. He worked to gain her cooperation.

She found that her hand was clutching his wrist and kept her eyes closed as she gave in to the tingles of excitement that coursed through her.

Next to him, she felt dainty, petite and desired. She had what she had come for, what would it hurt to take one night for herself?

He would be on to the next woman as soon as one crossed his path. Minerva had nothing to lose.

She opened her mouth and touched his tongue with her own. Her acquiescence sparked something in him.

He stroked her tongue with his, and the dexterity that his appendage had made her quiver. Her mind spun down a filthy path, and she pressed her hips against him. Her body had no doubt about the path it wanted to take.

The silk of her skirt and his trousers were no barrier to the heat coming off their bodies.

His mouth fed at her, and his right hand pressed her against him, covering most of her back with his palm.

She felt the surge of magic before it enveloped her, but everything went dark and she was too distracted to fight it.

The world brightened again, and he was holding her against him in what had to be his bedroom.

"What just happened?" Her body was still limp, and it was his hand and her corset keeping her upright.

"I relocated us. As romantic as it would be to take you under the stars, it would not be comfortable for you, and I would feel guilty for giving you pain."

She quirked her lips and felt the pull

of the swollen skin. *Damn, he can kiss.* "I thank you for your consideration, but the pause is a bit of a mood killer."

He sighed. "I thought as much, so I will give you this." He leaned toward her and exhaled.

Magic swirled into her and twisted around her. It was more of an aphrodisiac than anything she had ever experienced. She reached up and pulled his head down to hers, extinguishing the smile on his lips with her own.

He ran his hands up and down her spine, and her corset loosened. She found the closure of the belt that was supporting the wrapped fabric and opened it with a few short motions. The belt and the fabric rushed to his feet in seconds.

He broke from the kiss, spun her around and reached around her to open the busk of the corset. The rush of cool air against her silk-covered skin was enough of a sensory shock, but his hands covered her breasts, taking their measure with delicate slowness.

Her sharp inhalation shoved her breasts into his palms, and his measured squeeze demonstrated his appreciation for her curves.

She was just getting used to that touch when his right hand released her and shifted down her belly to press between her thighs. The silk became damp as he worked his fingers against her.

He stroked her, licked and kissed at her neck, and used precise strength on her breasts. She could hear her breathing echoing in the room and the whining moans mocked her as he took her senses to the edge of release before he set her free.

Her wail echoed back and muffled the wet sound of silk being torn.

He carried her to the bed, turned her and tipped her backward. She had just gotten her balance when she felt him parting her thighs and delving between them with his clever tongue.

The slick, wet thrusts brought her to the edge in a matter of moments. She twisted against his mouth, and he gripped her hips, holding her where he wanted her.

This time, the fire in her blood flared and held her in a stimulated state with her screams echoing and his tongue moving within her.

Minerva thrashed in his grip, and she gritted her teeth as she slowly ceased to spasm around his tongue.

He deliberately pulled his tongue out of her, licked his lips and went back in for a final long stroke. His smile was anticipatory as he straightened and eased her back onto the bed.

She had to let go of the sheet she was clutching as he slid her back so that he could join her on the bed. It wasn't an easy manoeuver. Her hands were knotted in the fabric and didn't want to release her one anchor to the world.

She looked over the ferocious expression and let her gaze slide down his body. The musculature looked as hard as the stone around them, to say nothing of his erection. In theory, all dragons were different in biology, but the dramatic tapering of the head of his massive cock was startling. It looked like it would pierce her before he got halfway in.

His grimace showed that he was watching her face. Without speaking, he reared back, slid an arm under her and flipped her to her stomach. Once he arranged her to his liking, he ran his hand under her, speaking soft words in a language that she didn't know, and she knew most ancient and extranatural languages.

As he cupped her sex, he ran his tongue up her spine, nibbling at her shoulders in turn. She quivered and sighed as her skin began to glow with heat again.

The words he muttered spoke to something in her, and she rocked her hips against his palm, inviting him to do more than simply caress her.

He groaned and trailed his tongue in lazy loops to the base of her spine. He moved in behind her and pressed the tight head of his cock between her folds, and the first few inches slid in easily because of the taper.

Minerva lowered her head and closed her eyes, biting her lip as he retreated and plunged in, deeper and deeper.

She rocked with him, taking him in as he slid and stroked every cell inside her.

He groaned and gripped her hips as he moved against her. To her shock, she felt his thighs against her ass, and he shuddered in a move she felt all the way through her.

The slow undulation began, and he leaned down, moving her hair away from her neck, licking and biting at her skin while he took his time working to his own release.

They rocked together for what felt like hours. He ran his hands under her, worked her breasts and stroked her clit. She was covered in sweat and grunting as he thrust into her. Her arms ached and trembled, her back and shoulders stung from the grazing of his teeth and claws, but her body's welcome still coated her thighs.

When the first twinges of orgasm struck, she froze. Her body tried to tighten around him, but she was stretched to capacity. She trembled and her breath caught in her throat, leaving her to shake and twitch as it gave way to pleasure once again.

Zemuel's cock began to move, but his hips were still pressed against her ass.

She gasped at the slow undulation, and when his hands tightened on his hips, his guttural shout echoed back to her.

He held himself against her, and when the undulation ceased, he slowly bore her down to the bedding.

It was like being flattened by warm stone. The slight yield of the bedding was enough to let her breathe but only just.

He slid a hand under her and turned them to their sides. He remained inside her and held onto her.

She squirmed and tried to ease away.

"Minerva, you and I have begun something that will not be undone." Zemuel's tone didn't brook argument.

She twisted and whispered a spell, building magic between them until he was locked in place and his eyes slowly drooped into sleep.

She eased off his cock and wasn't surprised to see it hadn't flagged. A lot of extranatural species carried it over into sex.

She gathered her clothing and checked on her victim one more time. She whispered the memory spell and transported away before he could see her and break her hold.

Home was not an option.

Chapter Five

Emile opened the door and smiled. "Minerva, how nice to see you."

He was wearing his human form, but his nostrils flared at her scent.

"Mage Ganger, I am in need of a place to stay. A heavily warded and off-the-map place."

"Come in, come in. Lenora will get you something to wear. Perhaps a shower?"

Minerva stepped inside. "Both sound good."

"Excellent. Head for the gold room. I will send Lenora up in a few minutes."

Minerva ran up the stairs with cum running down her thighs. Surprisingly, it was not her most humiliating entry into the Ganger home.

She couldn't believe her stupidity. The one time she let her hormones gallop away with her and she had to pick a dragon.

The shower took the traces of him from her, but the scratches and bites were still throbbing in her skin. The mirror was fogged, but she could see the red welts that Zemuel had left behind.

Sighing, she wrapped herself in a towel and entered the bedroom. Lenora came in with folded fabric and a smile. "I am guessing that it was a one-night stand?"

"I am hoping so. I didn't intend for it to happen, but he and I just fit so well..."

"Ah. What was he? Giant?"

"No. Dragon."

Lenora sat at the foot of the bed. "Which one?"

Minerva took the nightgown that Lenora held out. "Zemuel. I did some treaty work for goblins."

"Does he know where you are?"

Minerva scowled. "He did know a lot about me. I wouldn't doubt that he does."

"Well, you get some sleep, and if you don't want to see him again, we will work on a concealment spell."

"Thank you. I know that Mom's house is hidden, so that is a relief."

"Do you want me to call her for you while you rest?"

Minerva thought about it and then nodded as she climbed into bed. "Would you? She and I need to have a conversation, and at least, we are safe here."

"Rest, dearling. She will be here when you wake."

Lenora drew the shades and left her alone without any additional questions. That was what had made her go to the Gangers. Nothing in the realm of sex surprised them.

Lenora opened her door to Deirdre. "Good afternoon, Deirdre."

"Lenora, is she all right?" Deirdre looked frantic.

"She is fine. She is resting. Would you like coffee or tea?" Lenora smiled helpfully.

"Coffee, please. Is she safe here?"

"Very safe. Even she couldn't force her way in. She had to ring the bell, just like everyone else. They are the strongest barriers in the country, and she helped set them in place."

Lenora linked arms with Deirdre and led her to the kitchen. She set up the coffee press and waved her hand to boil the water.

Deirdre looked pale and her hands

were shaking. "Lenora, may I ask you a question?"

"Of course."

"Can the gods hear us here?"

Lenora sat at the table and took Deirdre's hands. "No."

She slumped in relief. "Good. I don't want them to hear what I have to tell Minerva."

"Is it about her being a demigod?"

Deirdre blinked. "Demi? Don't be silly."

Lenora's eyes widened as she caught on to what her acquaintance was saying. "I see."

"I have to tell her first. It is only right."

"Of course. She will be up around dinnertime. Will you stay?"

"If you will let me. I need to tell her what she is."

"Are they threatening you?"

"My goddess has my loyalty, but I

value my life. This is getting scary."

"Nothing to be frightened of here, and your daughter will see off any threats. She is not a woman to be taken lightly."

Deirdre smiled. "No, she isn't."

"You did an amazing job raising her."

"You did all the tricky work, Lenora. Try as I might, I just couldn't learn to do magic."

"You weren't touched by the waves, nor were your people. There is no shame in that. You are what you are, as Minerva is."

"Why is she here?"

Lenora smiled. "A lover's tryst got her more than she bargained for."

Minerva arrived, and she cleared her throat. "A lot more."

Lenora raised her brows. "I thought you would be out for a few more hours."

"Accelerated sleep spell. I got what I needed in three hours." Minerva went to her mom, kissed her cheek and then

headed to the counter to make the coffee. The kettle announced the boil just as
she arrived.

She poured the water into the waiting
press and set cups along with cream and
sugar on a tray. She carefully walked it
over to the table and had a seat.

Lenora smiled at the motions of the
woman who had spent nearly as much
time in the kitchen as Benny. "Well
done, Minerva. I will leave you and your
mother to your discussion."

Lenora got up, got a plate of cookies
and set it on the table next to them.
With her duties as hostess done, she left
her apprentice to the discussion of her
origins. She wondered if her suspicions
were correct.

Minerva got the coffee ready and poured

her mom a cup, setting the cream and sugar in just the way she liked it. "There you go. Thanks for coming. Today was a little unreal."

"You had a bad date?"

She wrinkled her nose. "Something like that. You know the kind of work I do."

"Of course. You negotiate between extranatural folk."

"Yes, and yesterday or possibly a few days ago, I met a man I felt attracted to, but he wasn't going to let me go easily, so I bespelled him and ran for it, so to speak."

"And you are afraid that he will come after you."

She shrugged. "If anyone could get through the wards, it would be him. Now, as we have been left alone for a discussion, shall we have it? What were you going to tell me about my origin?"

Her mother gripped her coffee cup

and sipped slowly. "It was a cold moon. I remember that much. The rest is a little fuzzy…"

"I can lift it from your mind as you think of it."

Deirdre nodded. "I think that would be best."

She walked to her small temple to the goddess of magic, and she knelt with her offering, placing the rare herbs on the altar and lighting the candles.

"Beloved Hecate, I beg for magic in my life. I am a hollow being without the touch of the energy that so many take for granted. Please, grant me magic."

She knelt there for hours as the moon moved above her. She was about to leave when she heard a small cry.

She looked at the altar, and in the place of the exotic herbs was a naked baby girl, wailing under the moon.

A woman appeared behind the infant

and more women appeared behind her.

The voice was in her ears, her mind and her soul. "Deirdre, we charge you with raising our daughter. We have created her from our own beings, and she is the magic that you seek. Take her to one of your places of refuge and apply to adopt her. We will make sure that you are the one to take this piece of us into your home."

Deirdre stuttered, "My ladies, I do not have the means to raise a child properly."

A bag dropped to the ground in front of Deirdre and gold spilled out.

"You may use it all and create a space that will honour our daughter and her new mother. Tonight is the day that you receive your magic, daughter."

A moment later and the goddesses were gone, leaving only the child and the gold behind.

Deirdre quickly took off her robes,

and she wrapped them around the baby. The infant smiled up at her with wise eyes, and Deirdre felt her heart thud until it beat for the little goddess in her arms.

Following directions, she took the baby to the local abandonment drop, leaving her wrapped and comfortable. After ringing the bell, the child was taken into the warmth immediately.

She was excited. The next morning, she went to a goldsmith and traded for a handful of the metal she had gotten. The money she received went straight into her bank account, and she was confident that the goddesses were looking out for their child.

A shockingly short wait and she had the baby in her arms again. It was like life was starting over.

Minerva blinked. She wiped tears from her cheeks. "Well, that was intense."

Deirdre smiled. "They did give me my magic."

"Do you know who they were?"

"Hecate, obviously. Over the years, I have heard the names of Rhea and Metis as well as Tyche, Psyche and the muse, Calliope. You were a group effort with each of them contributing part of themselves to you."

"Why do they want to talk to me now?"

Deirdre nibbled at a cookie and didn't meet her gaze. "You are a master mage now. It is possible that they want to set you to your purpose."

Minerva sat back and frowned. "Well, fuck."

"My sentiments exactly."

Minerva and her mother were in agreement, but what the hell could the goddesses want? There was really only one way to find out. She had to ask them.

Chapter Six

When there was no dragon in the skies above the Ganger home after two days, Minerva felt confident enough to go home with her mother.

If the goddesses wanted a conversation, she was going to make herself accessible.

It was best to get this kind of thing over with. For immortal beings, deities were fairly impatient.

She left her mother in the house and headed deep into their property. She went to the small temple and sat cross-legged on the floor with her mind open and her body relaxed.

"You are taller than I had guessed,

daughter." A woman with chalky skin and midnight hair stepped away from the wall.

"I am as I was made to be." She remained sitting.

Another figure stepped out of the shadows and then more. Goddesses finally surrounded her; waves of power filled the room.

She remained seated.

"Rise up, daughter. We would greet you properly." Hecate was amused.

With a sigh, Minerva got to her feet and faced the collection of ancient power.

An older, very tall woman stepped forward. "I am Rhea, and I gave you poise and your form."

A slightly smaller woman stood next to Rhea. "I am Metis, and I gave you wisdom."

A graceful woman smiled. "I am Psyche, and I gave you hope for love, a soulmate."

"I am Tyche; I gave you a grasp of fortune and fate."

"I am Calliope, and I offered you the ability to write and create."

"And I am Hecate; I gave you the floodgates of magic at your command."

"I am pleased to meet you, creators."

Rhea quirked her lips. "You do not call us mothers?"

"Deirdre is my mother. She sacrificed for me, watched me flourish where she had failed and held me and wiped my tears. I honour you as my creators, and I honour her for her sacrifices."

Metis nodded. "Wise statement."

"Now I must ask, creators, why did you bring me to life?"

Hecate smirked. "With the waves of magic in the world, I wanted another woman who could stand as goddess for the modern age, but I could not create her alone."

Rhea shook her head. "The first new goddess went mad. She had to be destroyed. Hecate chose Chaos as one of the contributors, and things went wrong. That would have been the great fire of seventeen twelve."

Minerva blinked. "Oh. Right. May I inquire as to my name?"

Tyche smiled. "Minerva oversaw our efforts so that none would overpower the offering of the others. You are equally a natural woman as you are a natural poet, creative writer, mage, lover, take your pick. No part of you wins out over the others."

"Good to know."

The goddesses came to her and embraced her. She didn't recognize what they said as they whispered into her ear, but part of her soul clicked into place with each contact.

She didn't grow stronger, but she felt whole.

Hecate came to her finally and kissed her forehead. "And now you will have whatever magic you wish at your command."

"Thank you, madam, I already do."

A hard hand gripped her chin. "You think you are clever?"

"I know I am intelligent, madam. It was designed into me. I believe that was Calliope."

Calliope cleared her throat. "Actually, it was."

Hecate looked at her with completely black eyes, and she grinned. "Good. You will need every bit of that confidence and intelligence. We are seeking our other daughters. They were not as balanced as you are. They are causing trouble."

Rhea crossed her arms and shook her head. "That is because Hecate thought that Chaos and Nyx would be good influences."

Metis sighed. "And Hera."

The crowd murmured in agreement.

Minerva raised her voice. "Wait. How many attempts have there been before me?"

Hecate muttered, "Seven. There are three still alive. Gods killed the others."

"Why?"

Rhea answered, "Childbirth. They wanted to plow the new goddess and start another pantheon."

Minerva winced. "Why was that a problem?"

Hecate shrugged, "Chaos wanted them to seek their own fame and fortune with no worries about family. They cannot have children."

Rhea smirked. "I did not make that mistake with you. You are built to care about those around you. That includes your family. Hecate had to agree that I could make you as human as possible before I would participate."

Minerva looked around. "They haven't come for me."

Hecate snorted. "You have hidden yourself well. Even we had to ask your mother to send you to us. If you had not come here, we would not have been able to touch you."

"That is... surprising."

Metis cocked her head. "Why?"

"You are goddesses."

Rhea laughed and Psyche smiled.

Psyche explained, "We have not been worshipped in over a thousand years in any way that matters. You were our last chance to make a mark on the world."

The other goddesses were silent.

"What do you mean, 'last chance'?"

Rhea came to her and placed a hand on her shoulder. "We do not have the power to do this again. We gave our all to you and made sure that you were taken care of. Even though Hecate will not admit it, she is proud of you."

"Why are you telling me this now?"

Psyche stepped forward and smiled. "We need you to find a champion. You are settled in your power and can defend yourself against most comers. After our gathering, the gods will look for you, and they will find you. It is old fashioned, but I would urge you to find a mate who will stand with you."

Images of Zemuel flashed through her mind. Psyche smiled. *"He might do. I am partial to men with wings."*

Minerva felt a blush rise in her cheeks. She didn't answer, but the goddess of emotion stroked her face.

"I need to think about what I have learned."

Hecate nodded. "You can summon us one at a time or all together. Just come here and ask. We will answer you."

"I have one request. May I give my mother magic?"

The gathering froze.

Hecate cocked her head with a smile. It was the first true smile she had exhibited. "You know how?"

"I am fairly sure. I merely want to give her power over her own gardens. They are her favourite place to be, and I believe she would enjoy it."

Hecate nodded. "If she agrees to it, you may give her the power over her gardens."

Minerva pressed her palms together and nodded to the goddesses. "Thank you, Mothers. I will endeavour to be worthy of your efforts."

Light surrounded her, and when she blinked to clear her vision, they were gone.

She let out a low and shaking breath, rubbing her hands down her thighs before she walked back through the woods to the house.

Her mother was waiting for her and gave her a cup of her favourite tea. The peach and strawberry flavours made Minerva smile. "Thank you."

"You look like you need it. How was it?"

"They are pleasant and appreciative of your efforts to bring me to adulthood."

Deirdre smiled and sat down at the counter. Minerva joined her.

She told her about the meeting and the conclusion.

"So, Mom. Would you like possession of enough magic to keep your gardens?"

Deirdre scowled. "I don't know. What would happen if I decided to make a plant bloom in winter?"

"It would die."

"Or change the colour of the flowers?"

"Only the ones you touched would change, and it would last as long as the limb on the flower lasted." She smiled. "You have a good grasp of this."

Deirdre sighed. "As much as I wish I

was born with magic, I wasn't. All the magic in my life, all that I have ever needed was in you."

Minerva teared up and went to hug her mother. They remained together for long minutes until they both retreated, sniffling and smiling. She might be adopted, but the way she dealt with the world was the result of the upbringing by a woman who knew magic when she saw it.

Deirdre smiled and wiped her cheeks. "Well, now. What I would like to have is the ability to know when you need me."

Minerva blinked. "That's it?"

"That is it."

Minerva got to her feet and went into the garden, grasping a two-inch river stone and turning it in her fingers.

She took it into the kitchen and headed to her lab. Some herbs for motherhood and communication and the stone would be ready.

Her mom came along and perched on a tall stool as she often did, watching Minerva with rapt attention.

The issue of Minerva being a goddess didn't even come up.

Zemuel woke and knew that something was wrong. He could smell a female on him and all over his bed, but no memory would come to him.

He wrapped some fabric around his hips and summoned Norman.

"Yes, Lord Zemuel?" Norman had his wings tight to his back.

"Who was my companion last night?"

"The Master Mage, Minerva Rogati. You were quite taken with her, and she with you."

Zemuel's lips twitched in amusement. "I cannot remember her."

"You have many video recordings of her. Perhaps that will jog your memory."

He rubbed his forehead. "She bewitched me."

Norman smiled. "If anyone could manage it, it would be her. I will fetch your laptop."

Half an hour later, Zemuel watched the recordings from his throne room, and he laughed at the expressions of those around her. She was a devastatingly impressive woman. Doubly so if she could bespell a dragon as old as he was.

He watched the subtle shift of her hips as she stalked to and from the bar. It was hypnotic.

"Where is she now?"

Norman cleared his throat. "I believe she is in Redbird City."

Zemuel groaned silently. It would take time to get an audience with Matthias. "Ask Matthias if I may enter his territory and clear my path with permissions."

"Yes, my lord." Norman was grinning, which was not like him.

"Why are you smirking?"

"If you want the lady's address, my lord, she left her bag when she departed."

Zemuel stared at him. "Her bag?"

"Her luggage. It has a name tag on it, complete with address."

He grinned. "Record the address and send the luggage to her via courier."

"Yes, my lord. I am on it."

Norman spread his wings and flew out of the centre of the building, heading for the nearest balcony to reach the guest tower.

Zemuel paused the video and zoomed in on Minerva's face. She had done a good job wiping herself from his memories. He would just have to learn her body all over again.

Thinking about her curves made him eager to get to Redbird City to meet with her again. His body still smelled of musk and honey. He wanted to taste her and see if his instinct was right. Was she as sweet as she smelled?

Chapter Seven

$\mathcal{M}$inerva was washing the dishes when she heard the knock at the door. Her mother was at the horticultural society, so she headed to answer the door.

The young male was dressed in a precisely pressed suit. He had two parcels, and he presented them with a smile. "Ms. Rogati?"

"Yes."

"These are for you. Courtesy of Zemuel. I was told to mention that you might have been missing the luggage."

She took her bag and felt the blood drain from her face. "Thank you."

"Oh, the other bag is from Mr. Norman. He said you might need it for the next time."

She set her carryon aside and took the box. "Thank you. Wait and I will get my wallet."

The young man held up his hands. "No. No need. Trust me, working for Lord Zemuel pays exceptionally well."

He bobbed a bow and turned on his heel, heading for the black sedan.

He hadn't just hired a courier company; he had sent his own man to deliver it.

She stood for a moment as if rooted to the spot before she retreated to the inside of her home. She was shaking as she brought the bag to her room and set the box down on her bed.

He knew where she lived.

Why hadn't she taken the luggage with her when she left?

She stared at the bag accusingly but then turned her gaze to the box. There was a wide black ribbon holding the box shut, and when she pulled it apart, a gown encrusted with jewels, embroidery and flowing silk lifted from the cardboard.

"Oh, my."

The fabric was a rich grey, and the pearls and stones were also in the same hue. The bodice was rigid, and when she flipped it over, the lacing up the back would leave a lot of her skin exposed. The skirt would throw her limbs into light shadow but not cover them. It was the opposite of what she normally wore. The opaque nature of her wardrobe was a matter of pride.

There was a letter in the box and a note. *As Lord Zemuel was not kind with your clothing, I offer this to replace it. Yours, Norman.*

She stroked the fabric and smiled before suspicion reared up, and she checked it for spell work. It hummed with energy, but it wasn't enchanted.

It had been six days since she had been with the dragon, and the memories still woke her with her skin flushed and her thighs slick.

She folded the gown back into the box and stroked it before she put the lid back on. It would just have to sit on her shelf until she got drunk enough before she went out to put it on.

Wearing that gown would be like wearing smoke. She wasn't sure how she felt about that, so she put it away.

How Norman knew about the shredded clothing was probably an educated guess based on Zemuel's past behaviour.

The box was tucked onto a shelf in her closet, and she grabbed her phone to check her schedule. She was going to take over for a friend at a magical supply shop and that would take up most of her next two weeks.

She loved playing with the ingredients. It was a chance to work on a few new personal spells that needed tweaking.

Minerva knew that she needed to write a thank you letter to Norman, but she would have to work out what she wanted to say. That was going to take some thought.

She grabbed her purse and her keys, heading to her small car. It would be a short drive to the shop.

Two weeks later, she was working in Sawberry's Magical Supplies when a familiar face came through the door.

Minerva grinned.

Sophy looked surprised. "Minerva? What are you doing here?"

Minerva smirked. "Oh, Tabeel drank some of her own tea and had to check into the medical centre. She will be fine as soon as she stops burping up fortune-telling bubbles."

Sophy looked at her and grinned. "When is she going to learn that she can't try her own concoctions?"

Minerva shrugged and turned to lift a wide box up and over her head.

The man with Sophy moved swiftly and helped her set it in place. Minerva looked up at him. "Well, hello. Friend of Sophia's, I presume?"

"You could say that. She is responsible for me." He smiled down at her with predatory interest. "However, if I had known that there was an enchantress such as yourself behind that wall, I would have beaten it down for the honour of your greeting."

Sophia rolled her eyes on the other side of the counter, and Minerva grinned. "You are not from around here, are you?"

"No. I am not. I am a very recent arrival, sworn to the service of the Cursed One."

Sophy snorted. "Nothing like the word *Cursed* to make a girl feel special."

He moved from behind the counter and returned to her side. "That is not what I meant."

"You are bound to me. I get it. Now, Minerva, can you help me out?"

Minerva held out her hand. "Give me the list, and I will tell you what is and isn't in stock."

"They should all be fairly standard."

Sophy retrieved the list from her ample cleavage and handed it over.

Minerva looked at the list and was amused by the male's attempt at chit-chat.

"How long have you known each other?"

Sophy snorted. "She is too young for you, Magnus."

"No. It just seems that you have a camaraderie that is surprising, considering what you are and what she is."

"What? That I am over a decade older than she is? Or is it that I tear magic apart and she creates it?"

As Minerva gathered items, he asked, "You don't know what her parentage is?"

She paused. She hadn't told anyone about it. It was just her and her mom. She hadn't even told Lenora yet.

Minerva focused on her job in the shop as she retrieved and weighed the list, piece by piece. Each item was placed carefully on a separate piece of tissue that would keep them from interacting before it was time. It wouldn't do to muddle the spell before it started.

Minerva tapped the list over and over as she returned to them. "You just need one thing."

Sophy looked at the list and blushed. "Right. I have that at home."

"Thought you might but wasn't sure if it was still good." Minerva folded the list with a smile. "Well, everything else is here."

She packed the items up, one by one, until she had a large bag and a smile. "Nineteen, please."

Sophy reached into her purse and pulled out a small coin canister. She opened one end and poured out the nineteen gold coins. "There you are. Tabeel should be happy. I think I just paid her rent for a month."

"Or, it will pay for her medical treatment. Either way, she will be happy. Have a great day, and we need to go for coffee at the Patchwork Dragon. It's illuminating."

Sophy grinned, and her eyes brightened with excitement. "Now that he isn't occupying it, my phone is at your disposal. Call me anytime. I will be only too happy to meet up. This is my first week off in years."

It was about the only thing that could have shocked Minerva. "You have time off? What happened?"

As the Cursed One, Sophy was always on duty. Minerva didn't remember her having a day off... ever.

Sophy chuckled and took the bag. "Call me when you are done here, and I will tell you over coffee."

"Done."

Sophy's man followed her out of the specialty shop, and Minerva started to breathe again. He knew. She didn't know how he knew, but Sophy's companion had sensed what she was.

She made a face and tidied up. Tabeel would be back in a few hours. Going out for coffee would be a piece of normal that she had been missing. Benny was married and working with the XIA, Freddy was still holding down her job at the online newspaper, Sophy had a day off and Minerva was going to take complete advantage of it.

The Patchwork Dragon was alive with customers. It was no wonder. Jennifer was an excellent seer, and a reading could be purchased with coffee if you were so inclined.

Sophy's male friend was sitting at a table of his own, and his gaze kept coming over to watch them. Minerva grinned at her and casually said, "He is staring again."

He was sitting with a sample of every type of coffee and tea available at the Patchwork Dragon in front of him. The table was covered with little white cups.

The servers were bickering to attend his table as he took sip after sip and made notes on a small piece of paper.

He was looking toward them with a hungry gaze.

"He is staring at you, Min. He and I have already had the talk that firmly lodged him in the friend zone. I am not his type."

Minerva chuckled. "You are nearly every male's type. Even the gay ones want to befriend you. I am pretty sure that you just got some signals crossed."

"I am pretty sure I didn't. Frankly, it was my virginity that put him off. He's repelled by it. Funny, right?" She sighed and sipped at her bowl of cappuccino.

Minerva scowled. "You are kidding."

"Nope. His mouth dropped open."

"I don't know what to say. Perhaps things were dif—no that wouldn't be right. A few hundred years ago, it was a prize."

Sophy shrugged. "I am used to rejection. Once folks realize what I do for a living, I am out on my own. It isn't something that most guys would sign on for."

"Well, I am currently dealing with a similar but opposing situation. I am used to guys running the other way, but an arms dealer is currently after me for sexual purposes."

Sophia blinked. "You are kidding."

"Nope. He is one of the mountain dragons. I was singing a few weeks ago to get a treaty ratified for the goblins, but when it was over, he invited me to dinner."

Sophia winced. "You didn't."

Minerva blushed. "I was hungry. It takes a lot of effort to maintain this figure."

"So, you ate with him, and then, he seduced you?"

She fudged the details a little to make her seem more adventurous. It was silly, but she suddenly felt the need to be more than the seduced. "Well, we had sex on the table. I excused myself afterward and made a run for it. The goblins were bound by a geas, and I didn't think he would be able to find me."

Sophy chuckled. "You do stand out, and they track by scent and taste. Body and magic."

Minerva grimaced. "I found that out when I did my research after the encounter. I haven't run into a dragon in a business situation before. It caught me by surprise."

Sophy thought about it. "Zemuel."

Minerva had a visceral reaction. Her fingers spasmed, she blushed and her breath caught in her chest. "How did you know?"

"Only so many dragons in North America. He is the only one with mines and property that the goblins would be interested in." Sophy chuckled. "I have worked with him before. He is a good sort, though he does like to collect mages around him. You would have gleamed like a diamond in sunlight to him."

Minerva groaned while Sophy sipped at a bowl. That explained his fixation. Well, at least she hadn't heard anything from him for the last few weeks.

They laughed, and Sophy gave Minerva some tips on how to handle a dragon with mating on his mind.

"You have to remember that he will be obsessed with the way you smell, the way you move and the magic in your body. If you are so inclined, you can drain power from him and he won't even care as long as he gets what he wants."

"So you are saying I should give in?"

"I am saying you already did, whether you knew it or not. If you truly connected with him, he isn't going to let you go. They can get sex anywhere. Mates? Not so much."

The proprietor was going around the coffee shop, reading cups and telling fortunes. When she got to them, Minerva smiled, needing the distraction. "Hiya, Jennifer. Business is booming."

The woman who looked a lot like their friend Benny smiled. "You can't beat the markup on coffee. Would you like a true reading?"

Sophy nodded. "Please."

Jennifer raised her hand, and a server brought Sophy another cappuccino. "Cradle it in your hands and take a sip."

Sophy she did as she was told.

When she put the cup down, Jennifer took it and focused on the foam and coffee.

"I see a man in your future, pure and impure. His mark is the spiral horn, but he fights his nature each day. Interesting. Another man with glowing power also calls to you, but he is driven by selfish desires and an urge to collect."

Jennifer blew softly across the surface, raising one hand above the coffee to hold the steam and read it. "You want but can't have. Desire but are rebuffed, and will not chase what you truly seek. You need a partner in all things, but the horned man is fighting you every step of the way."

Jennifer handed her cup back with a sigh. "You are screwed."

Sophy was startled into laughing. Minerva grinned; it sounded just like Benny.

Minerva's coffee was in Jennifer's hands a moment later, and Minerva's grin faded.

"You are being hunted, and he will catch you. The gods will come at your call, but you will have to choose, sunlight or moonlight, love or family."

Minerva blinked. "Right. Okay."

"Oh, and he will be here in five minutes, so if you don't want to deal with him, I would get going." Jennifer winked.

Minerva was on her feet in a moment. She smiled at Sophy. "Sorry, but I don't want to do this tonight."

Sophy waved her off, and Minerva ran for it with as much dignity as she could gather.

Five minutes wasn't a long time when she had parked three blocks away.

Chapter Eight

Minerva didn't know where she was going to go. She didn't want to go home. He knew where she lived.

She pulled over to the side of the road, and she called Lenora.

Emile answered. "Hello?"

"Hello, Master Ganger. This is Minerva. I was wondering if I would be able to use your wards today?"

"Is something after you?"

"Something, someone. I just need time to think."

She waited while he spoke to his wife. At their proximity to each other, she guessed they had been having sex. In the Ganger household, it was not an unusual activity.

"We will put you in the new guest-house. It should allow you the privacy you need."

"Thank you." She didn't ask when the guesthouse had come into being. With as much magic as the Gangers controlled, they could have brought up a palace overnight if they wanted to.

"See you in a few. Lenora is dying to know what has been happening over the last few weeks." He chuckled and the phone call ended.

It was with a sense of relief that she put her phone aside and got back on the road. She had a safe place to run to that he didn't know about.

The taste of Minerva's body was in the air. He followed the scent into the café and ignored the odours of beverages that tried to cloud his senses.

A familiar face was sitting at the end of the trail, but it was not the woman he was after.

He walked right up to Minerva's chair. "How much did I miss her by?"

The blonde simply smiled and sipped at her coffee. "Have a seat, Zemuel."

He narrowed his eyes at her. "Sophia DeMonstre? I haven't seen you since you were a teen."

"I know, but you make an impression."

When he sat, the chair creaked. He picked up the cup of coffee that Minerva had left behind. He flicked his tongue out and scowled. "I missed her by minutes."

"You did. She was out of here like a scalded cat. So, why are you stalking her?"

He flicked his bat-like wings and

smiled. "She's mine. She's perfect and she is mine."

He could see her judging his appearance and coming out with a favourable opinion, but she still set him straight.

"I know that you think so, but she is her own being first. Remember that when you deal with her. She is also powerful enough to take any appendages you have and turn them into innies."

He smirked. "I will keep it in mind. How goes your hunt for a mate?"

She flicked an imperceptible glance toward another table and shrugged. "I have only started."

"What about that mage?"

"Alaneus? He is after my pedigree. I need someone who can be a partner."

"Ah, interesting. That is a tall order. Your family has grown more powerful with every generation."

She smiled. "We aren't up to dragon standard, but we do all right."

She paused for a moment before she changed the thrust of the conversation. "I might start looking in the elves. They usually go after blondes with weirdly long lifespans and consistent youth."

He tried to imagine the hyper woman with a sober, eternal elf. It was an odd picture. "Invite me to the nuptials. I would like to see what you consider to be a good match."

She raised her bowl to him. "Keep me posted if you catch Minerva. She's a quick one."

He sighed in frustration. "I know. Her trail is gone now. She knew I was coming."

She wrinkled her nose in amusement. "There's a seer here. So, yeah, she knew."

He grimaced. A moment later, a cup shattered in the hands of a woman doing a reading for an extranaturally handsome man.

The woman looked at Sophy with wide eyes.

"I believe that is my cue to leave. I do apologize, Zemuel. All the ladies seem to be running out on you tonight."

"My ego can take it. Have a good night, Sophia." He reached out and kissed the back of her hand. He could taste the magic of her ancestors in her skin.

She blinked and smiled. "That never gets old."

"Good to know. Nice to know I still have moves." He winked and inclined his head. He sipped at the bowl of something that could have been coffee in a world made of sugar, and he leaned back on the creaking chair.

It had taken two weeks to get Matthias to allow him in his territory, and he was only allowed to find Minerva and leave. The king's new assistant had promised to intervene on his behalf and buy him some time, but he knew why the vampire didn't want him to remain for any significant period of time. If he created a nest, he would be bound to the land and that would mean Matthias would have to share power with him. It was not a situation that would appeal to either of them.

The frazzled woman with the broken cup sat at the empty chair. "Would you like a reading?"

He looked her over. She was brunette, petite and had the stamp of magic on her. It was peculiar; it was enforced from without and didn't bloom from within. She had been cursed with magic.

"If you could." He wanted to watch.

She nodded and flicked her hair over her shoulder, exhaling onto the surface of the liquid, and it heated again. Curls of steam rose and she caught them, examining them carefully. "You are looking for Minerva."

He blinked. "I am."

"You can find her if you ask politely." She flicked a glance at him, and her eyes spun with quicksilver.

"Would you please show me where I can find Minerva?" He leaned forward eagerly.

"It is not me that you must ask. Go to the home of the Gangers and ask for Minerva there. They are as close as family to her, and you would not be able to find them from the air. Knock and ask and be polite."

The woman shivered and smiled at him. "There. Heated it up for you."

He smiled in return. "Thank you. Do you have Wi-Fi?"

"Of course."

He pulled out his phone, and he looked up Dr. Emile Harcourt Ganger. Through cross-referencing, he found an address from fifty years ago, and he smiled, swallowing the last of the coffee before he left the café with a few hundred dollars on the table.

He returned to the car that Matthias had provided and gave the address to the driver.

"The Ganger home?"

"Yes."

He sat on the edge of his seat as the car rolled forward. It was not a traditional mate hunt, but if Minerva were the prize, he would do whatever it took.

The moment they turned onto the drive, he could feel the protective spells, the wards and the ancient magic.

The dowager house had a number of vehicles out front, but the sleek black vehicle continued to glide along until it was in front of the worn stone steps of the Ganger home.

Zemuel let himself out of the vehicle, and he walked up the steps, ringing the bell and waiting with his wings folded.

The scaled green features were familiar, and he grinned. "Harcourt!"

"I go by Emile now, but yeah. Wait, Zemuel, is that you?"

They clasped hands and slapped shoulders.

"Emile, who is this?"

The feminine voice was smooth to Zemuel's ears, and he looked past his old friend to the elegant woman walking toward them.

"Master Mage, Dr. Lenora Ganger, this is an old friend. Zemuel."

"Madame Lenora, it is an honour to meet you." He bowed low and took her hand in his for a moment before releasing it.

She smiled. "It is an honour to meet any friend of my husband's. Please, come inside."

He could smell Minerva. She was close, but her scent was even throughout the halls and building. She had been here and then left... or was there some-thing he was missing.

Tea was produced, and as the tray flew in and settled, Lenora poured for all of them.

"Cream or sugar?"

"Just sugar, please. Two." He inclined his head as she handed him the delicate saucer.

When they were all settled, Emile smiled. "Now, not that I don't enjoy see-ing you, but why have you come?"

Lenora's eyes were suspicious, but he was polite to both when he said, "I am seeking my mate. I believe she is in this city, and I need your help to find her. Will you help me?"

Emile smiled. "Of course."

"Emile!" Lenora tried to stop him, but the words were spoken before she could.

Zemuel sipped at his tea. It was quite good. "I am looking for Minerva Rogati."

Emile winced and looked at his wife

in apology. "Sorry, but he did have to come in through the door."

Lenora growled, an incongruous sound from such an elegant woman.

"Fine, but she is having a shower. I will go and get her in an hour. Do not worry, Zemuel. She is not leaving this property. I will abide by my husband's asinine promise. We will help you find your mate."

Zemuel inclined his head. "I have heard of the Ganger family since coming to Redbird City. I never connected it with you Har—Emile."

"I repented my wild ways and settled down with the only woman I could ever love, who would tolerate me enough to give me a child." Emile reached over and took his wife's hand, kissing the palm.

"Your daughter is recently married?"

Lenora smiled proudly. "She is in the XIA. Her team are her mates, and it is a good fit."

Zemuel raised his brows. "The entire team?"

Emile chuckled. "Vampire, elf and lion shifter. It is a good match, and she is my daughter."

Lenora jerked her chin up. "Minerva designed the binding spell."

"Which was compromised by some enchanted equipment, but it all worked out in the end." Emile nodded.

They sat and chatted about Beneficia and her mates for an hour before Lenora rose to her feet and left the room.

"Where is she going?" Zemuel nibbled on a cookie.

"She is keeping my promise. Don't worry. You will see Minerva in the next hour or so."

"Why so long?"

"I am guessing that Lenora will have to pry her fingers from the doorframe. Just a guess though." Emile grinned.

Zemuel sighed. So close and yet Minerva might as well be half a world away. Not that he wouldn't still find her, but though time didn't mean much to him, he was filled with an urgency that was hard to pin down.

If he wasn't sure that it was impossible, he would say that he was excited. He was far too ancient for that kind of foolishness.

Chapter Nine

Minerva was wandering around the new guesthouse when Lenora knocked. There was no doubt of who it was. The house shivered with her energy.

Wearing the fuzzy robe that the guesthouse had provided, she answered the door. "Lenora, what is wrong?"

"May I come in?"

"Of course."

She stepped aside, and her host entered, pacing up and down the living room nearly immediately.

"Spill it, Lenora."

"Zemuel is here."

Minerva felt her body go hot. "He is?"

"He is apparently an old friend of Emile's, and he believes you are his mate. Is there a reason for that?"

Minerva held up her hands. "We just had sex."

"I recognized his scent from that morning. Did you do anything or say anything that would indicate you had bound yourself to him?"

Minerva shook her head. "No. There wasn't a lot of talking to be honest."

"Mating marks?"

"Nibbles and scratches but no bites. I was healed up in two days."

Lenora smiled. "What do you think of him?"

Minerva blushed hot. "Uh..."

"I see. So, lots of hormones and not a lot of thought."

"Something like that. I just thought he would make a fun and enjoyable one-night stand."

"Did he?"

Minerva had to be honest. "Definitely."

Lenora cocked her head. "You knew he would come after you."

"I thought my memory spell would hold him."

"Did you remove all traces of yourself?"

Minerva winced. "No."

"Then, on some level, you wanted him to come for you. You are too experienced to think otherwise."

Minerva thumped down onto one of the couches. "I knew he would."

"So, you ran. Like a mate. You are making him chase you, and he has caught you, so to speak." Lenora came up behind her and placed a hand on her shoulder.

"What are my options here?"

"In this house, none. Emile promised his friend that he would help find the mate before we knew it was you."

Minerva grimaced. "Oh well. I will get dressed and go and meet with him."

"Good girl. You can always bespell him and run later. There is a family that made a tradition out of it."

Minerva nodded and headed to the bedroom where her clothing was draped over the edge of her bed. She flicked a spell that cleaned her underwear and got dressed. She wasn't heading into a room with Zemuel without underwear. Well, not again.

Dressed and steeled for the meeting, she linked arms with her master, and Lenora led her out, across the open field where the fey horses occasionally ran, though now, they hung out near the dowager house where Benny and the guys were living.

The path that led from the guesthouse to the main house felt like a road to her doom. She ruthlessly squashed the part of her that was feeling trills of excitement.

Her inner novel-reading teenager needed to zip it.

Once inside the house, Lenora nodded. "They are in the sitting room."

Minerva headed down the hall and looked into the sitting room. She muttered, "Not anymore."

She continued on and into the library. It was Emile's favourite spot, and he was showing his acquisitions to Zemuel.

The dragon turned the moment she came through the doorway. His smile was slow, but she could feel her mental block in his mind. He had sought her out without remembering everything.

"Minerva Rogati. I am pleased to meet you... again." He walked through the banks of tables and stopped in front of her. He bowed low and took her hand.

"Lord Zemuel, I am surprised you sought me out."

"Once I had caught your scent, there

was no stopping me. It was easy to do, it was all over me."

She blushed. "I knew I should have taken more time with the spells."

He shrugged, still holding her hand. "You panicked. I did as well the moment I knew I had met my mate and she had escaped. Norman had to remind me that I had surveillance footage of the meeting earlier that night."

She paled in horror.

He raised her hand to his lips. "My surveillance ends at the bedroom door."

She shivered at the touch of his lips against her. A thousand and one memories assailed her, and he smiled.

"I am really missing those memories if a kiss to your hand does that to you."

She licked her lips and cleared her throat. "Your memories aren't missing. You are too powerful for that. I just subdued them. They are still there."

He leaned down to her and whispered, "What will it take to wake them?"

She stared into his eyes, the silver of his face was completely unmarked by time, but his eyes showed that he had seen more than her lifetime had to offer.

"Uh. I could remove it now, but it would kind of rush in on you."

Emile muttered, "Take him to the guesthouse."

Minerva panicked. "What?"

"You broke him, you fix him. Those are the rules."

Lenora was in the doorway with a tray. "He's right. Those are the rules."

Minerva felt like her skin was radiating ice and fire in turn. The rules of the Ganger house had always been clear. If you used a spell that affected someone, you had better know how to undo it.

She was a little plaintive when she said, "Can I have some tea first?"

Lenora fixed her cup and handed it over. "There you go, precious."

Minerva scowled and took her hand back from Zemuel to take the tea. He didn't let go easily.

With the cup in her hand, she headed to one of the nearby couches and took a few sips of the hot brew.

The familiar taste relaxed her, and she settled into the seat while Zemuel watched her with amusement, and Lenora got Emile his cup.

Zemuel came to stand next to her. He crouched down and smiled. "I will not jump on you the moment the suppression comes off."

She looked at him glumly. "That is what you say. I have done this kind of thing once before, and it ended up in a fight that nearly killed him."

He chuckled. "I can take whatever you have to give, little goddess."

She froze. Lenora and Emile looked at her in surprise. "Why did you call me that?"

He sipped at his own tea. "I have met many goddesses in my time. You radiate with that particular energy."

Lenora had a weak smile. "Did you know?"

Minerva nodded. "I haven't had a proper chance to tell you."

Zemuel looked to her master and Emile. "You didn't know?"

Lenora smiled. "I knew she had power and abilities beyond standard magecraft. I did not know she was born to be a deity."

Minerva made a face. "How could you know? I was adopted. It wasn't like my house was shaped like a temple."

Emile cocked his head. "Do you know your origin?"

"I do. It is a bit private though." She glanced at Zemuel.

He nodded. "I will leave you for a few minutes. Do not doubt that I am staying close."

He snagged a cookie on his way past the tray and closed the doors to the library behind him.

Emile and Lenora came close, and Minerva explained the goddesses and the incarnations they appeared in.

"Well, the titan portion explains your height."

Minerva chuckled at the observation. Apparently, she hadn't changed in her master's eyes. "I suppose so. Rhea took great pleasure in my physical appearance."

Emile nodded. "You are an impressively built woman. If I didn't have Lenora, I might have tried my luck."

"And I would have blasted you back to the demon zone, but it is a good thing that I think of you as aunt and uncle." She winked.

Lenora gave Emile a sharp elbow. "Yes, good thing."

Minerva laughed and she sighed. "I

don't feel like anything else. I mean, I still feel like me."

Lenora stroked her cheek. "I am guessing that you have been a goddess all along."

"Thank you, Master."

"You are welcome, Master." Lenora chuckled. "Now, go and put the dragon out of his misery. Stealing time from him was not well done of you."

"You recognized it?"

"I know the symptoms. Shoo."

She got up and set her cup back on the tray. As she straightened her shoulders and opened the door, she heard Lenora murmur, "Do you remember when I did that to you?"

Emile chuckled. "Not until your master made you reverse the spell."

Her tutors laughed together at close proximity. Minerva knew that sound. She was going to have to leave the house anyway. Things were about to get loud.

Zemuel was standing still in the hall with his eyes closed. As she stepped toward him, his eyes snapped open and she closed the library doors behind her as laughter and murmurs increased in volume.

"Come with me, Lord Zemuel."

"I will follow you, Mage." His lips quirked in amusement at the formality.

She turned and headed out the back door, across the deck and down the path. She didn't say a word until they were in the new guesthouse.

She waited until he was inside and she had closed the door, shoving the coffee table out of the centre of the room.

"Kneel here." She tossed a cushion down for him, and he looked at it in amusement.

Minerva put her own cushion down and knelt.

He ignored the cushion and knelt in front of her.

She sighed. "Probably better this way. Are you comfortable?"

He shrugged. "I am used to hard surfaces."

"Right, well, do you want the spell removed slowly or quickly?"

"What is the difference? Pardon, but I am not often bespelled."

She blushed. "Right. Um... slow will be an easing of the memories back into your mind. Fast will dump the entire night into your thoughts in one burst."

"Slow then. I want to enjoy each memory as it surfaces."

She blushed and closed her eyes, muttering the spell swiftly. When she finished, she opened one eye and he was looking at her expectantly.

"Damn. I must be missing something. Just a moment."

She closed her eyes again and ran over the circumstances of the first spell. "Oh, damn."

"Is there a problem?"

She wrinkled her nose. "I cast the spell while we... while you... damn."

"What is the issue?"

"You were inside me while I cast the spell. That is the missing component. The physical connection."

He grinned. "I believe that we could re-enact that."

She thought about it for a few seconds, and then, she stood. He watched in surprise as she stripped to the skin.

Before she could lose her nerve, she knelt on the cushion again, and she said, "If you would slide a finger into me, that should be enough for the spell. I would have taken one into my mouth, but I need to be able to speak."

His wings lifted slightly, and he leaned forward, running his fingers across her breasts and down her belly. He drew designs on her skin as his digits got closer to her sex, and when he parted her lower lips, she gasped.

He thrust his finger into her, and they groaned in unison.

She clutched at his arm and started muttering the spell again. This time, his eyes widened and she could feel the block peeling away.

Chapter Ten

She whispered the chant to keep it echoing and moving through his mind, but it was difficult as his finger was also moving inside her.

His gaze was distant as he relived their verbal foreplay. She knew when he got to the kiss, because his lips caressed hers. The spell had enough momentum now; it was cascading through on its own.

Stroking his tongue with hers seemed natural considering the occupation of his hand. She sighed against his lips as he stroked her clit with his thumb, and she dug her nails into her palms. She tracked his memories, and when he reached the moment when he slid into her, Zemuel backed up.

He pulled his finger from her and stood up.

Aching and frustrated, she watched as he stepped away from her. To her surprise, he wasn't taking his memories and leaving. He was stripping.

The form he was wearing was his most human. At six foot six, it was as close to human as he could get, but his wings were still manifest. Those who didn't know what they were looking at might have mistaken him for a gargoyle, but the silver of his skin didn't look like anything other than metal.

The feel of him wasn't that of icy metal; there was nothing but heat when he touched her.

He wrapped his arms around her and lifted her from her kneeling position. "I told you that something had begun that would not be undone."

Her face was nearly touching his. "Careful. That is when I zapped you."

He grinned and walked toward the bedroom. "I will risk it."

Her feet dangled off the ground, and his erection was pinned between them. She didn't ask how he knew where the bedroom was. He could probably smell it.

Dragons were an exercise in the senses. Smell, hearing, touch, taste, each sense helped them keep their hoard safe. Sight was nice, but the others warned of danger long before it came into view.

He settled her on the bed and smiled. "This is familiar."

She leaned up on her elbows and cocked her head. "Is it? I don't remember you being this chatty."

He let out a chuffing sound, deep in his chest, before he parted her legs and pulled her knees up, widening and opening her in one move.

His wings extended, blocking out the light from the windows. All she could see was Zemuel, and he nudged her folds with the head of his cock before sliding inside.

She arched her back and groaned as he moved into her in increments. He was nearly inside when she bucked and let out a coughing moan.

"It would sound so much better in my bed, but I will take it." He leaned down and nuzzled her cheek.

She turned her head and kissed him. He delved into her mouth as he thrust completely inside her.

The slow rock of his hips against her was a beat she wanted to remember.

Sweat gleamed on her skin, and she raised her hips to meet his. He braced himself on his arms and continued to kiss her slowly as they mated.

Minerva ran her hands over his arms, shoulders and back. She stroked the hidden edge of his wings, and he thrust deep.

She lifted her legs and locked them at the base of his spine, pulling herself onto him as he slid into her.

He groaned into her mouth and pulled her hands away from his back, pinning them above her head as he thrust hard and fast.

Her peak rushed up and swamped her. She shrieked against his lips, and he shuddered against her, jerking his hips in short pulses.

He slowly lifted his head, licking at her lips, kissing her cheeks and brow.

"That, I want to remember." He smiled and met her gaze.

His expression was nine shades of satisfied, and his eyes were gleaming.

She twisted her wrists in his grip. He let her go.

Minerva stroked his cheek. "I don't know how this can work."

"I believe we just proved that it can."

She threaded her fingers into his hair. It felt like feathery down.

"That wasn't what I meant. My friends, my family, my contacts are all here."

He nuzzled her cheek. "I can have a fixed portal set, or we can move to my place in Corudet City. I should probably spend more time there, but there has never been a reason to settle in."

She blinked. "You actually have a place in the city?"

"Several. I am the mayor or king or something. One forgets after time."

Minerva stared at him. "This is going to require some logistics. I don't know how it will work."

"Do not worry. We have time. The child will not arrive for another eleven months."

Minerva stiffened under him. "What child?"

"You are pregnant. I knew it the moment I saw you here. You quickened at our first meeting."

She squirmed and bucked under him, but he seemed to have tripled in mass. He just waited until she got tired.

He was amused. "Now, now. That isn't good for the baby."

Minerva frowned and slumped back. "How can you be sure?"

"Well, your scent has changed, and a small marking has begun just above your pubic bone and is spreading upward. When it completely covers your belly, it is ready to come out."

She tried to look down, but his belly was pressed to hers. "That is bizarre."

"The wave changed me as it killed many in my village. I spent my first few years flying and seeking out others of my new kind. Two had mates, and this was their indicator."

Minerva blinked at the conversation

she was having with him still inside her. "You were near a wave point?"

"My village was split in two, and the survivors were all changed. Now, you would state it as ground zero. We absorbed magic that would not be seen again for centuries."

"Where did you meet the gods?"

"When they were ready to leave their community and hide in the human world. Several chose death, but others scattered."

"I have been warned against the surviving gods."

Zemuel scowled. "Why?"

"They want to make another pantheon, and they need a new goddess to do it."

He smiled slowly. "They can't have you. You are mine."

"I am my own." She narrowed her eyes.

Zemuel started rocking against her,

slowly delving deep with every inward thrust.

"I will agree that you are your own, but I am claiming the right to defend you and be your only lover from this point onward."

She gasped, and he threaded his fingers with hers, kissing her softly as he moved inside her.

No words of denial worked their way through her lips, only small sounds of enjoyment managed to escape. When the fire growing inside shattered into waves of pleasure, she sighed and flexed her fingers against his. His groan was soft, and he moved his lips from hers and pressed them to her shoulder. His bite was soft, but she felt the sharp teeth pierce the skin.

She held perfectly still as the teeth went deeper and deeper, but he released her a moment later as he scraped his tongue over the wounds. She could feel the magic in his slow, wet strokes. Power was working into her skin.

It took her a few tries, but she managed, "So, were you planning on getting off me any time soon?"

"No. I plan to stay here forever."

She sighed and wiggled her hands free. She put her palms on the balls of his shoulders. "That isn't going to work for me."

He wrinkled his nose. "You still think like a human."

"I was raised human... mostly. I have a human mother, humanish friends. Time is still a concern, because they are in my life, and time is a major factor in the human world."

Zemuel sighed and slowly lowered his head to her neck, licking and kissing his way down as he retreated down her body and withdrew from her sex with a wet sucking sound.

To say she was appalled when he

pressed his lips to her bruised sex was an understatement. He slid his tongue into her, and once again, she felt waves of healing magic emerging from his appendage and working into her abraded tissues.

She shook and held onto the sheets as fire skimmed along her nerves, but before she could go over, he pulled back and licked his lips. His smile indicated that he knew what he had just done.

She sighed and slowly sat up. He helped her and held her against him, rubbing his hand up and down her back.

"You have enthralled Norman, by the way. In his eyes, you have always been a goddess and you should dress accordingly."

Minerva leaned against him. "I know. He sent me a gown, but I have no idea where to wear it."

"We will have to find an occasion. There are a few invitations that Matthias had for me when I arrived. Folk that wish to see me and a display of magical artifacts that he loaned to the museum. It is a good place for a date, I think." He smiled.

"You... we... a date?"

He chuckled. "The courtship involves me winning your favour each and every day we are together. I do not want a running mate."

She raised a shaking hand to her hair. "I don't think I could walk right now, let alone run."

He smoothed his hand over her back. "I should not be smug now, should I?"

She elbowed him, and he flexed his wing around her, supporting her like an upright hammock with the texture of chamois leather.

She wiggled her toes and waited for her limbs to come back under her control. "I don't know what to do with you."

He chuckled. "I can suggest a few

things."

She stroked a hand on his thigh. "I bet you could."

He shivered slightly. "Never mind. I am pretty sure that it is something we will grow into over time. Just know that I will come when you call."

She stretched and groaned at the double entendre. "Speaking of calling. I need to call my mother. If I don't introduce you right away, I am going to hear about it."

He perked up. "Would you like her to live near us?"

"Well, yes, but I don't want her to move if she doesn't want to. She enjoys gardening and meeting with garden clubs, but I have no idea what your city can offer in that regard. You should ask her about it."

"Will I meet her soon?"

"As soon as I can get cleaned up, we will head over there. She will want to know what has happened and that I don't have to dodge you anymore."

"She was concerned?"

"She was terrified for me. It is one thing for me to adapt to what the goddesses said and another for me to deal with a dragon in pursuit because I flashed some ankle."

"I was interested in your cleavage, not your ankle."

She grinned and nudged him. "Come on. Let's get a cab and go meet my mom."

"Matthias has provided a car for me."

"Even better. Just give me a minute to get dressed." She levered herself upright.

He got to his feet and smiled. "I suppose for the sake of human modesty that I should get dressed."

"Please. My mother isn't extranatural."

"I will be on my best behaviour.

Promise." He winked and gave her a quick kiss before he left her to retrieve his clothing.

She used a cleansing spell to tidy up as she walked into the living room to get dressed. He was quicker than she was and watched her slowly hide the skin that he had been so very enthralled with.

"I will enjoy seeing you in clothing more appropriate to that of my mate."

She gave him a dark look as she zipped up her jeans. "Yeah, that isn't going to happen."

Chapter Eleven

Deirdre poured tea for them and looked Zemuel over. "So, you are a dragon?"

"Yes, madam." Zemuel was being very polite. It was adorable.

Minerva had changed clothing when they arrived. Too much magic use tended to build up in cotton. Her jeans were ready to spark into something disastrous. She was going to have to soak the magic out.

The loose maxi dress she was wearing was comfortable and suited to the weather.

"What kind of dragon? I can't do much reading in the magic books, but I know there are different kinds."

He sipped at the tea, the cup ridiculously small in his fingers. "I am a stone dragon. Or earth if you prefer. My kind sleep for centuries under the ground and keep an ear out for what is going on in the human world. When we hear something interesting, we wake up."

"Oh. How long have you been awake?"

He paused and tilted his head. "Four hundred years? I arrived before the colonists and settled into my home. I carved my home in the cliffs and then set about preparing Corudet City. I had no idea it was near a wave point until a century later."

Deirdre gasped. "You are kidding."

He leaned forward and whispered, "I am not. The ground cracked open in the centre of the city and energy poured out in a wave that spread outward like a pebble thrown into a pond. The ripples went on forever, and then the population showed up."

Minerva was enthralled. "I knew it produced a lot of transporters, but I didn't know it was a wave point."

"Before the colonists, only those who had been at the wave could record it. I have tomes full of amazing extranatural occurrences in my library. I have always loved collecting books." He set his teacup down and snagged a cookie.

"You collect books? What kind of books?" Minerva leaned forward.

"Histories. I have always been fascinated by histories. It is not enough to live the moment, but having you write it down and tell it from your point of view is essential. It makes the history come to life. It gives the moment a soul that allows it to live forever."

His passion for the written word was obvious, and Minerva was shocked to share it. His holding court like an ancient monarch hadn't really given her the thinker vibe.

Zemuel quirked his lips. "To use the vernacular, you thought I was a dumb jock?"

She blushed, and it was answer enough. He chuckled.

Deirdre smiled at the interplay. "Minerva would ride my corpse down the mountainside for a book."

Zemuel was still amused. "I do not think she would be so extreme, but it would be a near thing."

"You have not seen her in a studying frenzy. When she needs to look up the basics of a spell, there is no stopping her. She consumes every bit of knowledge and then goes looking for more. The Gangers have accused her of having perfect spells."

"She does seem to go after everything with focus."

She watched as her mate and mother

seemed to be getting along fine. It was surprisingly touching. Deirdre offered him a tour of her gardens, and he took the offer immediately.

Minerva sat and watched the odd couple wander through the pathways that Deirdre had so carefully tended over the decades. He paused and asked questions that her mother gracefully answered. It was adorable.

Minerva was doing the dishes when her mother came into the kitchen. Zemuel had left for the evening, heading to his lodgings at the mayor's home.

"He seems nice."

The amused and dry tone made Min laugh. She put the last of the dishes away and sighed. "He wants me to move."

"He told me. He offered to set me up with a garden three times the size of this one... and bees."

Minerva snickered. "Wow, he knows how to get a mom on his side. What did you say?"

"I said I would have to see it to believe it."

Minerva grinned. "Way to hold out, Mom!"

Deirdre hugged her. "He is a good partner for the destiny you are walking toward. He will be there when you need him."

Minerva hugged her mom in return. "I am pretty sure he will, but where are you going to be?"

"Baby, you are a goddess. You are not going to age and wither. I will."

"Don't talk like that."

"I will talk any way I please. I am going to get old and fade away. I am just hoping that I will get to see a grandbaby before then."

Minerva froze. "About that..."

Her mom leaned back. "What?"

"Apparently, it is possible, in some strange stretch of the imagination and peculiar timing, that I could be pregnant."

Deirdre blinked. "When will you know?"

"I don't know. A month or so?"

"I had better learn to knit." Her mom hugged her tight again.

Minerva rested her chin on Deirdre's. Her mom was right. It was going to be hard if she was actually sculpted of ancient magics. Deirdre was going to be a great grandmother, but she would flicker and disappear in a few decades.

She never wanted to let her mom go.

Zemuel stepped out of the car and smiled to his driver. "I will check in. You do not need to watch me."

"I am under orders to follow you until you are back under Matthias's roof."

Zemuel walked to the door, and it was opened before he could touch it.

The butler nodded and said, "This way, please, Lord Zemuel."

Zemuel followed the creature through the halls and into a large private office.

Matthias was at his desk, and his assistant was at hers. Leo was working and making calls. The vampire king smiled as Zemuel stepped forward. "So? How did things go?"

Zemuel sat on the backless bench that had been set out for him. "I believe I have made progress."

The mayor of Redbird City snorted. "You are radiating satisfaction. I think progress was definite."

"She is more than I was expecting."

From her desk, Leo snorted. Matthias's assistant had a highly amused expression, but she kept working.

Zemuel looked back at his host and smiled. "It seems that there is a consensus."

The vampire king folded his hands on his desk. "You seem uncertain."

"Do you know of any wandering gods in the area?"

Leo's head snapped up. "That's a thing?"

"Leo, please pretend you aren't hearing this. I will explain it all later. No, Zemuel, there are no wandering gods nearby, but there are high incidents of summoned ones in the vicinity."

Zemuel nodded and asked, "If that offer to the museum gala is still open, I would like to attend with Minerva."

Matthias nodded. "Easily done. Leo?"

"Am I listening now?"

Matthias rolled his eyes. "Yes. Can you put Zemuel and Minerva on the list?"

"Already done. Even booked their

driver. Anything else?"

"Have you looked into nursery schools for your niece?"

She wrinkled her nose. "Of course. Mind you, my sister doesn't seem inclined to get back to work. Her flirting with the guys has taken on epic proportion."

Zemuel sat there while they discussed the merits of socializing the little girl with folk other than extranaturals. To his amazement, he realized that he was going to be having a similar discussion with Minerva one day. His grin was more than a little foolish when Matthias returned his attention to him.

"She's pregnant." Matthias chuckled.

"All signs confirm it. How did you know?"

"I have seen that expression thousands of times. I hope, for your sake, it isn't a girl. Leo's niece, Melody, is still an infant, but already, she takes up a lot of space and time."

"I look forward to the challenge." Zemuel smirked. "All I need to do is convince Minerva to move in with me. How difficult could that be?"

Matthias and Leo cackled for a solid five minutes.

Minerva checked out her belly in the mirror, and there, under her navel and just above her curls, was a small tendril of colour. A small silver vine with a tiny leaf was curling upward.

"Well, hell. Hello, junior. I wasn't expecting to see you, but now that you are there, welcome to your start in the world."

She patted the small mark and felt the tingle of magic run through her fingers. There was power there, and it would take the entire gestation period before she found out if it was residue from its parents or belonged to her baby all on its own.

She slipped on her robe and went into the living room. Her mother was sitting with a book and a cup of herbal tea.

"What is it, sweetie?"

"Tell me about how you managed having a baby with magic."

Deirdre smiled.

Minerva sat next to her mother for the next three hours and listened to how one went about diapering a baby that could levitate, as well as how one kept a child eating healthy when they could summon their favourite cake.

When Minerva went to bed, her mother tucked her in like she used to and pressed a kiss to her forehead. "Zemuel had better build me an impressive garden. I need to be a proper grandma to the little one. Oh, and I am going to need a new temple to the goddess."

Minerva smiled as her mother stroked her cheek. "Make a list."

They laughed together, and despite the creepy circumstances, both were pretty happy with Minerva's choice.

Chapter Twelve

$\mathcal{I}$t was a definite plus that the gown Norman had sent over covered her nipples. The jewels covered the important bits, but the translucence hinted at everything else.

Her mom helped her with her hair, and magic held it in place. Minerva hated pins.

The doorbell rang, and Deirdre smiled at her. "That is probably him."

"I hope so, because I am tempted to order pizza and stay in." She turned from side to side, looking at the dress that was part elegance and part tease.

It was just luck and a bit of enchantment that made her shoes a perfect match.

Her mother returned and smiled. "He's here, Minerva. Have a nice time."

She nodded and headed for the door. The appreciation and admiration in his expression made her surprisingly happy.

"Good evening, Zemuel."

"My lady, you are radiant." He bowed and his wings lifted slightly.

He was wearing a tuxedo that was slit to accommodate his wings, and the fit was perfect. "And you are striking."

He took her hand and brought it to his lips for a kiss. "Thank you, but I pale in comparison to your beauty."

She took in his added height that evening. "Are you taller for a reason?"

"To defend your strength and beauty. With a woman such as you at my side, I will need to be on alert."

Minerva smirked. "Nice call with the strength comment."

He released her hand and offered her

his arm. "I wasn't born yesterday."

Her giggles continued as they settled into a stretch SUV, and it pulled away from her mother's home. She felt like she was going to prom.

While Minerva had attended any number of formal gatherings in the past, she had never gone with a date. This evening was new territory for her.

The driver took them through town and to the museum.

When they arrived, Zemuel exited and came around to help her out of the vehicle.

She took his arm for stability as they walked on the thick carpet to the entrance of the museum. A few camera flashes blinded her, and Zemuel flexed a wing, wrapping it around her and keeping them from taking more pictures.

Spots dance in front of her eyes as they stepped into the building. "Thank you."

"I am not a fan of appearing in news reports and tabloids, but they got enough of you." His murmur was meant for her alone.

He presented two heavily embossed invitations to one of the security personnel, and the head curator escorted them through the halls and into the exhibit.

Daggers, cups and instruments of torture were only part of the exhibit. Ancient portraits and documents were of interest to Minerva. She saw a silvery dragon in one of the images and sought out a few others that had the same tiny beast in the distance.

"Is that you?"

He leaned in and checked the dates. "It is possible. I was in the general vicinity at the time. Wait, let me check on that."

He leaned until he was nearly touching the image. "Yes, it is a depiction of me. I remember this artist. She did a number of portraits in my home."

"She was a friend." Minerva was surprised.

"She was. Her story was tragic, and I knew her only for a decade."

"What happened?"

He gave her a sad smile. "Elsinor disappeared as silently as she appeared. One day she was out in the centre of the field, and ten years later, she disappeared from her studio in the tower."

"Were you lovers?"

He chuckled. "No. She was firm on that point. I was not invited to her chamber and did not invite her to mine. She was a friend and companion, and I still miss her."

"Do you think she lived a long life?"

Zemuel sighed. "No, but I think she is alive today."

"That doesn't make sense."

"You have lived with extranaturals

around. It makes sense if you look at it a certain way. I don't know where she is, but I am sure she didn't live long, and just as certainly, I am sure she still walks the earth."

She reached down and squeezed his hand. She looked past Zemuel and spotted a dark-haired woman smiling at her. A moment later, the woman disappeared behind a cluster of people. There was something about her. It was as if she wanted to be seen but didn't want to engage.

Minerva shook her head slightly, and they continued touring the exhibit. If the woman didn't want to speak to them at this event, it would have to wait for another day.

The mayor and his assistant were holding court. Leo's skill at dealing with unruly vampires was already legend in Redbird City.

Minerva had met Leo a few times in

the last few months, and she was a polite and no-nonsense woman. It was an excellent foil against Matthias's calm and brooding nature. She got things done; he thought about them. Together, they were unstoppable.

Leo's calm demeanour made her an excellent assistant for the mayor. When surrounded by thrashing and hungry vampires, she didn't get scared, she got angry.

Minerva smiled at her. "This is quite the event. The artifacts are wonderful."

Matthias turned and smiled. "Leo picked them out. She has an excellent eye for what will draw the public to an event."

Zemuel observed, "Not a lot here from your early days."

"I was more concerned with survival then and far less with storing parts of my life for later admiration."

Zemuel smirked. "And yet, I see several items from a period only a few centuries later."

"Well, there is nothing wrong with going around to collect your past. I spent some time seeking out relics during the Middle Ages. They were venerated and easier to find then. My collection is in the Corudet Museum."

"I think I would like to see that."

He smiled. "I would enjoy showing you."

Zemuel and Min walked through the exhibit together, and Minerva could feel the glances that they were drawing. She didn't mind. Zemuel was the one catching most of the stares.

Minerva was surprised to see Lenora and Emile looking at the exhibits. Her mentor smiled. "It seems you have worked things out."

"It is coming along."

Lenora tugged her away from Zemuel and led her to a parchment outlining the first vampire settlement in the new world.

"Min, how are you feeling?"

"Fine. Why?"

"I have been reading the omens. There are eyes on you. Focuses that weren't there last month."

Minerva smiled. "Have you been checking up on me?"

"Of course. I check on Benny, you and Freddy regularly. I did my second doctorate in scrying, you know."

"I know. So, what do the portents say?"

"Just that dark powers will seek you out. I have no idea what the outcome will be. There is a block there." Lenora huffed in frustration.

Minerva patted her mentor's hand. "It will be fine. I am aware of my surroundings, and if someone picks a fight, I will be ready."

Lenora sighed. "This has been a

rough year. I would hate for anything to happen to you or the baby."

"How do you know about that?"

Lenora smirked, "I was looking into your future. Didn't you hear that part?"

Minerva sighed. "This is getting weird."

"You don't feel it yet?"

"No. I can see the mark, but my body feels the same."

"Give it a few months. You will feel the changes." Lenora winked.

Minerva sighed and looked around. A few members of the gathering were looking in their direction, and one startling male had eyes that were solid black. He gave her a slight smile, and when she looked at him, he disappeared. No one around him even noticed, so she guessed she had been looking at a projection.

She was going to have to mention increasing the security protocols to the curator. If someone could project in, that was sloppy warding.

Four hours and two dozen hors d'oeuvres later, she curled up against Zemuel's side as they were driven back to her home.

A note on the kitchen table said, *I have gone out with Lima and Deara. I will be home in the morning. You have the house to yourself.*

Zemuel chuckled. "That is very accommodating of her."

Minerva looked at the note. "This is wrong. She hates Lima, and Deara died six months ago. Something has happened to my mother."

He paused. "May I see the note?"

She nodded. He lifted the paper to his nose, sniffed it and tasted the ink.

"Deirdre was afraid when she wrote this, but why would someone take her?"

Minerva took the page to her workshop, her gown rustling as she moved.

Zemuel reduced size to follow her. "What do you think has happened?"

"I think someone has taken my mother. I just don't know why."

She set the page on the table, got a few bottles down and poured a pinch of revealing powder into her palm. With careful fingers, she sprinkled the dust over the letter.

Zemuel didn't ask what she was doing.

She followed the one powder up with one for enhancing emotion and another for tracking.

When she was done, she covered the page with her palms an inch from the surface. She muttered the words of focus and activated the powders one at a time.

The paper curled at the edges as whatever had taken Deirdre fought to hide. She flicked aside their barrier, and she got the images she needed flowing through the air ahead of her.

"She is still on the property."

Minerva nodded. "They took her to the temple."

"Before we go and get her, how are your healing skills?"

"Excellent. Why?"

"Bring what you need in case they have injured your mother."

She nodded and grabbed a belt that she filled with tiny vials. It clashed with the gown, but she didn't give a fuck at this point. They had her mom.

They moved silently through the back yard under a cloaking spell. It took a lot of effort to hide Zemuel. His signature stood out like a firebrand.

The kidnappers had obviously thought that they would take the opportunity to be alone, because they ran into one of them on the path to the temple.

Zemuel stepped forward, grabbed the

man and suffocated him until he dropped. Minerva had discussed it with him. If these guys were gods, they would give up power when they died. It was best to incapacitate them without killing them.

The crack of the leg bone made her wince, but it didn't wake the unconscious man. He wouldn't be following.

Zemuel returned to her side, and they continued on their journey to the temple in the woods. No other men got between her and the small building, but she heard raised voices when she got there.

"I did not go through all of this for you to kill off my acolyte, Zagreus." Hecate was angry.

"I have been reborn, built by the gods as your new daughter was. I am destined to rule, and I will have a new pantheon to keep the humans in their place. What is one worshipper among the millions that will follow?"

Zemuel stiffened at her side and made a gesture to where he sensed Deirdre. She nodded, and they walked up to the temple, seeing her mother tied inside with panicked eyes and a gagged mouth.

She was lying in front of the alter in a perversion of the herbal sacrifices she normally made.

Minerva was furious, but she channelled her inner calm and dropped the concealment around her only. "Lady, Zagreus, Mom. It is an odd gathering for such a late hour."

Zagreus jolted, his black eyes wide. It had been his projection at the museum that she had noted. He tried to cover for his surprise.

Zemuel was outside the temple, hidden from all senses. If Minerva hadn't been holding the edges of the spell, she wouldn't have known where he was.

Deirdre started to cry, but she kept

her chin up. Minerva had never been more proud of her than she was at that moment.

The god looked behind her, and he frowned. "Where is Mercury?"

"Oh, was he the guy on the path? He had an accident."

Zagreus stepped toward her. If she hadn't been hanging out with a seven-and-a-half-foot dragon all night, she might have been slightly intimidated, but his six-foot-six muscled frame couldn't compare with Zemuel.

She lifted a finger, and he was stopped in his tracks. He could not take one more step toward her.

Hecate looked at her in surprise.

"Daughter, I think it would be in your best interest to give in to Zagreus."

Minerva looked at Hecate and kept her expression blank. "No. I give in to no one. You may go, Lady Hecate, if you wish to come out of this unscathed, but know that I will not forgive you for this betrayal."

Hecate looked at Zagreus, and she disappeared. Whatever was in Minerva's face was enough to tell her she had definitely erred.

Zagreus stopped trying to approach her. He turned and lunged for Deirdre.

Zemuel got there first; he ripped the back of the temple open with one giant claw and scooped Deirdre carefully into his embrace.

Minerva wished she had been able to watch him transform fully, but there would be plenty of time for that later. Now, she needed to deal with a petty god.

She stepped toward him. "Did you think I would just fall on my back with my legs open?"

Zagreus tried to bully her. "You are a young goddess. You don't know the power you can wield with a little tutelage. I can give you that."

"No. I do not need anything you have to offer. Now, prepare to defend yourself."

He stared at her and made a final push against her barriers.

She swatted him back with casual disdain. She pulled two vials from her belt and flung the contents at him.

He flinched and flailed. "What was that?"

"Oh, a little cocktail I have been working on. Blood from a demon banished to the demon zone, and a spell to send you there in three, two, one, bye!" She waved cheerfully as the ancient god was sucked through a portal and it closed behind him.

She felt the flicker of energy as the broken god left her mother's property.

Minerva ran out to the space where Zemuel was guarding her untied mother in his claws and under the shielding of his wings.

"He's gone, Mom."

Deirdre got up and sobbed, running to her. They hugged for a long moment, and Minerva looked at the proud and lizard-like head of her mate. His body was huge, and from nose to tail, she guessed that six city buses would have to be used as a measurement.

His skin had the mirrored texture of mercury, and she could only smile at the beauty of his form.

"You are lovely, Zemuel."

He lifted his head and wiggled it at her compliment.

"I need to get Mom somewhere safe. Do you know of a place?"

The eye she could see lit up, and he bowed his neck. Minerva coaxed her mother into place where neck met shoulder and scooted in behind her, casting a warming spell and a securing spell as he launched into the sky. They were snug, warm and together. She trusted Zemuel to take care of the rest. Corudet City was about to become home.

Epilogue

"Mom, thank goodness you have come." Zemuel seemed genuinely relieved.

Deirdre smiled. "What can I do for you, son?"

The wedding had been small but every extranatural being had been there when her daughter had wed the mayor-king of Corudet City. He insisted that she call him son, and he called her mom. It was weirdly cute.

"She won't come out of the library. She keeps muttering that she has to be ready in case anyone attacks again, but she isn't eating and hasn't slept in days. It can't be good for her."

"Or the baby."

"She is more important to me." Zemuel scowled.

Deirdre stifled a smile. "Have you tried taking her books away?"

He looked a little sheepish. He held out his hand, and the marks were evident. "She bit me."

Deirdre pressed her lips together and patted his arm. She passed him and headed down to the research library that Zemuel had gifted Minerva with. It was a dangerous wedding gift. Deirdre knew how her daughter was around books and had been sure that it would cause an issue for Minerva to have exposure to unlimited knowledge.

The doors opened at her touch, and she walked in and looked for her daughter in the dim interior.

First things first, Deirdre went to the windows and opened the shutters, flooding the space with light.

The hiss told her where her daughter was, and she finished opening the windows and letting fresh air into the library. There was a distinct funk in the room, and it was coming from Minerva.

Zemuel was in the doorway but not coming in. It was better that way.

She hopped up on the table next to the books Minerva was poring over with her eyes glowing white.

"Hey, honey. I just thought I would let you know that with Zemuel's help I have gotten a new temple underway in the centre of town."

Minerva blinked rapidly and her eyes dimmed. "You are still worshipping Hecate?"

"Oh, no. It is for you. Minerva of Corudet, goddess of education and magic."

Minerva put her pen down and looked up at Deirdre. "That is stupid."

"I know, but we have to start somewhere, so I thought a local temple would be a good thing. Folks have already started praying. I am guessing that it is what has been driving you and keeping you from noticing that two weeks have gone by and you haven't showered or eaten."

Minerva blinked and sniffed. "That's me?"

"Oh, yes. Now, go and take a shower, have something to eat and a nap, and I will tell you about the scholarship programs that you are funding and the request that the Mage Guides have for your appearances."

Minerva got to her feet and swayed. "Mage Guides?"

"Yup. Little girls who want to talk to you about careers in enchantment. I am hosting a support group for human parents who have extranatural children."

Deirdre eased Minerva toward the door, and she swayed and stumbled the entire way to Zemuel.

Deirdre watched her daughter look up at her husband. Minerva whispered, "You should have told me I was obsessed."

He caught her gently in his arms. "I tried. You bit me, so I called your mother. Mothers are handy things."

Deirdre watched as her son-in-law carried her daughter off for a bath and some food. Mr. Norman came up to her and offered her his arm. "Lady Deirdre, if you would come with me, I have prepared lunch for two on the terrace."

Deirdre grinned. "Sounds delightful, Norman."

Of course, Corudet didn't just hold the promise of love for her daughter. The perks of dating a gargoyle were just beginning to make themselves apparent.

She had prayed for magic in her life, but she had gotten so much more than she imagined.

Author's Note

So, there. Minerva's story. Next, we will deal with Freddy and her life as a hellhound.

Hellhound in a Handbag tells the story of Freddy, her attachment to her mage and a bid for freedom that could kill her... hope to get to it soon.

Thanks for reading,

Viola Grace

About the Author

Viola Grace (aka Zenina Masters (aka Viola Masters for dark erotica)) is a Canadian sci-fi/paranormal romance writer with ambitions to keep writing for the rest of her life. She specializes in short stories because the thrill of discovery, of all those firsts, is what keeps her writing.

A writer who crafts a story that catches you up, whirls you around and sets you down with a smile on your face is all she endeavours to be. She prefers to leave the drama to those who are better suited to it; she always goes for the cheap laugh.

Listening to readers has gotten her this far, and with her 300th short story behind her and 400th in the near future, she will continue to listen.